DEATH AND THE MOGUL

A Brace Heller Novel

R. Scott Bolton

Copyright 2023 by R. Scott Bolton
ISBN: 978-0-9997962-5-2

A Rough Edge Studios Production
www.roughedgestudios.com

Other books by R. Scott Bolton

From the Adventures of H. B. Fist
KILLED BY DEATH
OVERNIGHT SENSATION
BURNER

Brace Heller Novels
KNIFEPOINT
BEGIN RUMBLE STRIP

Standalones
DEAD DICK
NEATH: THE STORY OF A HAUNTING

For Leo
Who made our lives better every day.

.

As always, thanks to my ever-vigilant Quality Control Team. The readers listed below offered opinions and corrections that helped form the completed work, and I can never thank them enough for their input. But I'll try: Thanks to Shelley Bolton, Josh Bolton, Doug Bolton, Sue Bolton, John DeRuvo, Denise & Joe Lopiano, Steve Snider.

Also, a special shout-out to the National Novel Writing Month non-profit organization. Each November, they challenge their participants to write a novel in thirty days. I started in 2013 and have completed the first draft of a novel every year since. DEATH AND THE MOGUL was one of those. I heartily recommend NaNoWriMo to anyone who is considering writing a novel, screenplay, stage play or whatever. NaNoWriMo helps keep you focused. Check them out and feel free to donate: www.nanowrimo.org

CHAPTER ONE

Someone was watching me. I could feel it. I could sense their eyes on me as though their lashes were tickling my face. It was like having the red dot of a laser targeting device suddenly appear directly over your heart. You knew someone was out there and you knew they were probably up to no good. And your skin tingled with that knowledge. Warned you. Prepared you to be ready for anything.

I was at the desk in my office on the corner of Main Street and California. Second floor. The waiting room was empty. The front door was closed. If there was somebody in the hallway, I couldn't see them. The only sound was that of the mid-morning traffic on the street outside.

Earlier, I had tilted open one of the upper windows, knowing that it was going to get hot again this afternoon, especially for November. It was 11:12 AM. The expected heat had yet to arrive, but the air had a thick, thermal feel to it. It was probably a perfect 75 degrees at the moment, but it would edge up to 85 or even 90 by three o'clock. I wanted to be out on the streets by then. Down where I could find a cool breeze and maybe a glass of frosty beer. But that all depended on how much work I got done this morning. I looked down at the desk. A blank computer monitor and a silent phone stared back at me. There was no work to be done. At this rate, I'd be out of there by noon.

But I could still feel those eyes on me, beseeching me, begging me, daring me to return their stare.

So, I did.

"Wurzel," I said to the dog sprawled out on the plush doggy bed on the floor near the small office refrigerator. "You gotta go potty?" Any other time I would have felt silly using baby talk, but this is the proper way to talk to dogs.

Wurzel's big brown eyes widened in pure, unadulter-ated joy and he sprang from his bed, his back feet paddling so quickly that the doggy bed shot out from beneath him. He managed to keep his balance, planting his feet on the slick tile floor, and propelling himself in my direction. He danced at my feet, made little yip-yip noises in the back of his throat. He couldn't stand still. He vibrated. His nails tap-danced a skeleton melody that echoed throughout the office.

I walked over to the hat rack, removed the leash that was hanging there, and slipped the harness over his head. The latch clicked in place, and I tugged on it, making sure everything was secure.

"Sit!"

He did.

"Let's go."

We did.

We walked down the stairs to California Street (Wurzel had an unexplained fear of elevators and the one in our building was too slow anyway) and stepped outside. Immediately, the soothing, saline scent of the Pacific Ocean filled my nose, and I took a deep, refreshing breath, savoring it.

We turned right and headed toward the beach. I could see the deep blue of the water just a few blocks away. The sun beat down on us but not obnoxiously so and there was a mild breeze traipsing lightly through the streets that dried the perspiration on my forehead away with a gentle coolness.

Traffic was mild but that would change soon enough as the lunch hour approached. Downtown Ventura had become just a little bit famous for its eateries in recent years and, in addition to the usual local crowd, the restaurants were frequented by a sea of eager tourists. Based on my experience, no one was in for any disappointment.

We stopped at a crosswalk, and I punched the button with the back of my hand. Wurzel pulled, tightening the leash, but relaxed when I gave him a little tug. "Good boy," I said.

"Frenchie?" said a voice. I turned my head to find a young couple standing beside me, both just a little overdressed for the weather. Visitors, probably. I gave them a sunny Welcome-To-Ventura smile.

"Boston Terrier, actually," I said, nodding down at Wurzel.

"Really?" said the male visitor. He was wearing Bermuda shorts, a Champion Spark Plug t-shirt and, white socks and a pair of sandals made by a manufacturer I didn't recognize. Had they been Tevas, he could have been dressed as The Shorts and Sandals Detective for Halloween. Except for the socks. Never wear socks with sandals.

The unnecessary OREGON DUCKS zip-up sweatshirt he wore looked uncomfortable, but he seemed fine with it.

"With those big ears?" he asked, eyeing Wurzel at the curb.

I nodded. "They're just big ears," I said. "But he's a Boston. I've got the papers to prove it."

"Really?" the man asked again.

"Really," I said. "But that's not the first time he's been mistaken for a Frenchie."

"I bet," said the man, and stepped into the street as the light turned green. "Have a nice day."

"You, too," I said, following him into the crosswalk.

Wurzel and I continued toward the beach, passing The Habit Burger Grill (the smoky scent of cooking burgers made my mouth water instantly) and, across the street, peeking out from behind a Chevron gas station, Barrelhouse 101. I knew that Barrelhouse 101 had an amazing selection of beers and that they were pet friendly. Seemed that Wurzel and I had a stop to make on our way back from the beach.

We crossed Thompson Boulevard and took the California Street bridge over the 101 Freeway to Harbor Boulevard. Wurzel was straining at the leash now, anxious to get to the sand to take care of his business. We reached the promenade with its parade of tourists, bicyclists (most on rented bikes), and homeless persons and threaded our way through to the stairs that led down to the sand.

I checked my pockets. Yes, I had poop bags.

Wurzel nearly dragged me down the cement stairs and lurched forward, leash as tight as a guitar string, until he found his spot. He crouched down like a linebacker and let go. I turned my head to give him a little privacy and found the typical beach police eyeing me. People on blankets and under umbrellas watching me closely to make sure I picked up the poop. I pulled a plastic bag from my pocket and gave it a little dramatic wave. Some of the watchers turned away, satisfied. Others did not, hoping that I'd leave Wurzel's waste where it fell, so they could have a little fight.

I didn't give them the opportunity.

I scooped up the poop with the plastic bag and proudly deposited it in an overflowing nearby trash can. Most of the lookie-loos stopped looking. One or two did not. Probably not their fault. It's not often you see as perfect a specimen of manliness with his nearly-as-perfect dog on the beach.

We stood on the beach for a moment, basking in the sun's warmth, enjoying the cool ocean breeze, and listening to the laughs of children and the jovial rumble of the ocean waves. The day was pure and clear, and you could see the Channel Islands jutting proudly out near the horizon. Blankets and towels were scattered everywhere, some shaded with open umbrellas, their occupants taking in some golden rays. Others were vacant, their owners perhaps enjoying the cool ocean water. The beach was crowded but not so much that you couldn't turn over without disturbing the family on the blanket beside you. My eyes followed the jutting wooden shape of the pier from the taco shack closest to the freeway to where it ended 1,600 feet out at sea. Dark silhouettes moved about on its boardwalk, some with fishing poles tilted over its rails, most just taking a walk, some of those hand-in-hand.

It was another beautiful day in my hometown. Life was good.

I felt my cell phone vibrate in my shorts pocket before I heard it ring. Wurzel gave me a look as if to say, *Really? You're going to answer the phone on my walk?* I dug out the phone and glanced at the screen.

MELISSA PATTERSON.

I frowned. I wasn't expecting a call from Melissa. I hoped everything was all right.

I slid the answer switch to the right and put the phone to my ear. "Melissa, it's Brace," I said. "What's up?"

"Hi, Brace," Melissa said, and I could sense a tone of frustration and pain in her voice. "Do you think you could come over? I may need your help with something."

"Give me half an hour," I said, already heading up the cement steps to the promenade. Wurzel followed obediently but I could see the sad look in his big brown eyes as his afternoon at the beach was cut short.

Chapter Two

Melissa Patterson and her husband Mark had been friends of Marina's before she and I had even met. Melissa and Marina had gone to high school together. Mark was a cop who had worked with Marina on some of her more disturbing Social Services cases: child abuse, elder abuse. People who had become threats to themselves and perhaps to others.

We had double-dated once or twice when Marina and I first started seeing each other and I liked the Pattersons. They were smart, friendly, and quick to laugh. Happy people. As time wore on, the double-dates led to occasional dinners at each other's homes, Thanksgiving celebrations and Superbowl parties. I wouldn't say that Mark was my best friend, but we knew, liked and respected one another. That accounts for something.

When Mark was shot and killed by a junkie attempting to escape a convenience store robbery, Melissa received all the help she could get from the Ventura PD, including his pension, a large insurance settlement and the promise that whenever she needed help, someone would be there. But when Melissa needed help, it wasn't the VPD she would contact first. Instead, it was almost always Marina. And because Marina would do anything for her friend, that went for me, too.

So, when Melissa called that sunny Monday morning and asked me to drop by her place in the Ondulando neighborhood, I knew she was in some sort of trouble.

Ondulando is a group of homes that sits on the hills of Ventura, overlooking the city itself and offering some of the best ocean views in the state of California. They are some of the most sought-after homes in Ventura County, as their pricing proves, but they also run the risk of being burned down every ten or twelve years when the wildfires burn through the hills. Most residents there say the trade-off is worth it.

I pulled the Camaro to the curb in front of Melissa's house and shut off the engine. It was quiet up there and I just sat a moment, listening to the cooling tick of the big V8 engine. Through the windshield, I could see the wide-screen CinemaScope image of the Pacific Ocean stretching from one side of the glass to the other. It was no wonder people pay a fortune to live up here.

I climbed out of the car and double-checked to make sure the wheels were turned properly for parking on a hill. Marina had drilled it into me: Parking downhill, wheels to the curb. Parking uphill, wheels to the street. I felt a flash of pride surge through me as I noted the front passenger-side tire was gently kissing the curb there.

The front door was cracked open about four inches when I stepped up and I turned my head to listen. The frantic sound of TV cartoons came to me from somewhere inside as well as what I deduced to be the sounds of some-one cooking. My knuckles rapped three times on the open door.

After a moment, Melissa arrived, wiping her hands with a kitchen towel.

"Brace!" she said. "Thanks for coming."

"Of course," I told her. She opened the door and stepped onto the porch, trapping me in a brief hug.

"Come in, come in," she said. "I'm just making some tacos for Stevie. You want some?"

The tacos smelled delicious, but I passed.

"Do you mind if I finish up while we talk?" Melissa said.

"Of course not."

Melissa busied herself about the kitchen, the savory scent of simmering ground beef taunting me.

"I need your help, Brace. I did something stupid.

"We all do."

"It's not *all* my fault," Melissa said. "But I knew better, and I got caught."

"Tell me."

"The other day I ran to the grocery store," Melissa said, using a spatula to shovel tortillas on and off the grill. "I took Butch with me because he looked bored, and I worry about him sometimes spending all that time alone."

"Butch?"

"Our dog," Melissa said and then laughed. "Oh! You probably haven't met Butch. I got Stevie a dog. Seemed like a good idea with everything that happened. You know, a companion. For Stevie."

"It is a good idea," I said, thinking about Wurzel, now at home, alone himself. "Dogs are good companions. What kind of dog is he?"

"He's a Yorkie," Melissa said. "A Yorkshire terrier."

"Cute dog."

"He's a good boy," Melissa said. "But here's where I screwed up …"

She lowered her voice and peeked down the hall toward the living room, where the cartoon sounds were coming from. She apparently didn't want Stevie hearing what she had to say.

"Okay," I prompted.

"I left Butch in the car when I ran into the store. I only need a few things: bologna, eggs, some cheese. Brace, I couldn't have been in that store for more than five minutes, ten at the most. But when I came back out, Butch was gone."

"Gone?"

"Gone."

"He got out?" As much as I loved Melissa, I was really hoping she hadn't called me out here to find her lost dog.

"No," Melissa frowned. "That's the thing. When I left him there, I lowered the windows a bit, you know, so he could breathe. Not enough so that he could get out. Just enough to give him some air."

"Sure."

"But when I came back out, the driver's side window was open almost all the way. And there was a note."

Alarm bells went off. "A note?"

"Yes. A note saying that my dog had escaped but they had rescued it. There was a phone number on the note, too."

"And you called?"

"I did. They told me they had Butch and had been taking care of him, but they lived out in Oxnard. They told me they'd give me the address for $200."

I growled. "Bastards."

Melissa nodded. "They told me if I didn't pony up the $200, they'd just take him to the pound."

I sighed and shook my head. "That's a shakedown," I said. "It's basically dognapping. Everyone leaves their dog in the car. Everyone leaves the windows down. These crooks, they force your window down, grab your dog, and leave the note. There was a ring that did that a few years back. They eventually got shut down by the police." I gave her a look. "But they didn't take the dogs to the pound if you didn't pay. They knocked them over the head and buried them in the back yard."

Melissa gasped.

"Don't worry," I said. "I'll get him for you."

Melissa stopped what she was doing, wiped her hands on her apron and went to the table, where she dug through her purse. "I was hoping you would," she said, pulling out a wad of cash secured with a binder clip. She tossed it on the bar in front of me.

"What's this?" I asked.

"Two hundred dollars," Melissa said.

"No, screw that," I told her. "We're not going to pay them."

"Yes, we are, Brace." She pushed the money closer to me. "I don't want any trouble. I don't want you to come to any harm." She smiled. "I don't want Butch to come to any harm."

"No one's going to come to any harm."

"I'm serious, Brace. I just want to pay them the money and get my dog back. I mean, if something happened to you, Marina would never forgive me." She took a breath. "And if something happened to Butch, Stevie would never forgive me. I don't want to take that chance."

I stared down at the money. It looked like ten twenty dollars bills, folded together, all clipped with a big black metal binder clip.

I nodded. Picked up the money. "I'll try not to use this …"

"The hell you will," Melissa said. "Just give them the money, Brace, and bring me my dog." She held up her finger as I opened my mouth to protest. "Seriously, or I won't give you the address."

I shook my head. "Melissa …"

"Promise me. Just pay them and get my dog."

I took a deep breath and reached for the money. "I hate this," I told her. "We're basically paying ransom."

"I know."

"I mean, Puño and I could go down there, get the dog, shut them down, save you $200." Puño was six foot, five inches and over two-hundred and fifty pounds of pure Mexican fury.

"I know."

I frowned. "But you don't want that."

"I don't. I don't want anybody to get hurt. I just want my dog back." Her mouth softened. "I just want Stevie's dog back."

I tucked the wad of cash into my cargo shorts. "Okay," I said. "We'll do it your way."

Melissa went back to the stove, shoveled some ground beef into a couple of tacos, and then took a little taste. She made a pleased face.

"They're good," she said. "Sure you don't want one?"

I smiled. "I'm sure."

Melissa stepped into the hall and called toward the living room. "Stevie! Your lunch is ready, hon."

"Just a minute, mom!" came Steve's voice. I could hardly hear it because of the cartoon noise which, I now realized, wasn't cartoon noise at all. Sounded more like a videogame.

"How's he doing?" I asked when Melissa came back into the kitchen.

"He has good days and bad days," she said. "He misses Mark, and sometimes he acts out. There have been a couple of minor incidents at school but, for the most part, he seems to be getting better."

"Time heals all wounds," I said, and immediately felt stupid for saying it.

"Not all wounds," Melissa reminded me.

I nodded slowly.

"Well," I said. "I guess I'm gonna go get me a dog."

Melissa gave me a smile of gratitude. She went back to her purse, dug around again, and came out with a Post-It note. She passed it to me. There was a phone number and an address written on it in black marker. Saratoga Street.

"Do I need to call or something?" I asked. "Make an appointment?"

"No," Melissa said. "They said just show up, give them the money, and they'd give me the dog."

"He got a tag or anything?"

"Of course," she said. "It's got his name and my phone number on it."

I shook my head again. "If you needed any further proof these people are crooks, there it is. Why leave a note? Why not just call you later using the info on the tag?"

Melissa nodded. "Because they wanted me to know they took him," she said. "They wanted me to know that he hadn't just jumped out of the car and got squished beneath a truck or something."

"Makes sense," I said. "Bastards."

Chapter Three

Saratoga Street was about a twenty-minute drive from Ondulando, located out near the Oxnard Airport. The street was a collection of predominantly decent family homes, the front yards of most surrounded by inexpensive chain link fences and gates. Some of the homes had been converted to two story structures; most had not. The yards were well-kept, except for a few and those few that weren't maintained were hideous. A couple looked like a platoon of gophers had moved in, tunneled throughout the expanse of the lawn, killed the grass, and made the yard their own personal rodent condominium.

There was one lawn so bad that even the gophers wouldn't touch it.

What little grass there was in this lawn was dead, sticking up stubbornly in little tuffs of brown or yellow. Most of the yard was a patchwork of dirt and litter. The only green on the entire lawn were weeds, most standing proudly more than a foot high. I could see everything from tattered plastic shopping bags to crumpled fast food wrappers to drained automobile oil cans tossed about helter-skelter. There were a couple of dark spots that indicated something had been buried there at some point and I didn't want to think about what exactly that might be. A rotting GMC pickup—a vehicle that might have been quite the thing in the late 60s—rested in the middle of the yard, covered in dust and spider webs, and rusting so badly that pieces of its fenders had simply rusted away and fallen off. Its deflated tires were nothing more than rotting rubber, spilling off its motionless wheels like cooling lava.

Of course, it was the same address as the one written on the Post-It note that Melissa had given me.

I parked the Camaro across the street (just in case that GMC rust was contagious) and watched the house for a few minutes. There was no indication that anyone was home. The tattered drapes were closed, and I could see no movement through their Swiss cheese holes. The grey Nissan Sentra parked in the driveway was so dusty I couldn't tell what color it was. It was like looking at a black-and-white photograph.

For the first time, I found myself wondering if I should have brought along Puño for back-up regardless of what Melissa asked me.

I climbed out of the Camaro, made a production out of locking the doors, and stepped across the street. The long driveway gate squealed like a murdered pig as I scraped it open. If someone was home, they knew I was there.

And then I heard the dogs.

There were a lot of them. Barking, whining, crying, fighting. I was almost certain I heard a painful canine howl. Most of the noise was coming from inside the house but I was aware of dogs barking in the back yard, too.

I walked past the Sentra and took the crumbling path that led to the doorway. The dog sounds were louder now, and I thought I could see some activity through the holey curtains. I could smell them as well. That many dogs produce a lot of dog shit. I didn't want to go inside that house if I didn't have to.

I reached for the doorbell but changed my mind at the last minute and knocked instead. Something told me that a house in this state of disrepair didn't boast a functioning electronic doorbell.

It was less than a minute before the door opened, and someone peeked out at me from behind a security chain. The sounds of dogs became a roaring din and the sour stench of dog shit and piss rolled out at me like a wave.

"What do you want?" said the man inside. He was wearing a pair of filthy blue jeans, a stained white sleeveless t-shirt and muddy white socks, no shoes. His face was doughy and puffed out like a biscuit. I could tell from the lack of focus in his eyes that he'd already been at the beer … or something a little more potent.

The house inside was dark. No lights were on, and the curtains were drawn. Somebody forget to pay the bills?

"I'm here for Butch," I told him. "The Yorkie?"

The man blinked, turned to look behind him, and then hollered. "Butch? Yorkie?" I heard someone respond in the positive in the darkness and the man turned back to me.

"Yeah, we got him," he said. "You got the money?"

I pulled out Melissa's wad of cash and held it between my thumb and forefinger. "I got it," I said.

The man reached out to snatch it, but I pulled it away.

"Dog first," I said.

"It don't work that way."

"It does this time."

The man blinked again, a sleepy, not-quite-there blink, and then gently closed the door. I heard people talking inside and, after a moment, the door opened again.

"She's getting him," the man said. "Gimme the money."

"When I have the dog," I said.

The man's shoulders fell in disgust, and he turned around again. "Hurry up, Lacey! Bring me that fuckin' dog!"

The door closed again, and I heard the security chain rasp in its slot. Then the door opened all the way and suddenly the man was there again. As the sunlight filled the interior of the home I could see a wall of wire cages, one atop another, filled with unhappy dogs.

A gray woman in an ancient Tracy Chapman "Telling Stories Tour" t-shirt (that should have been converted into a shop rag years ago) walked up behind him. The tiny Yorkshire Terrier in her arms looked up at me with terrified eyes.

"The money," said the man again.

"The dog," I said, and wiggled the bills.

For a split second, the man seemed to consider saying no but then thought better of it. "Give him the dog," he said, stepping back. The woman took a step forward and reached out, pushing the Yorkie into my arms. He snuggled against me, and I could feel his tiny heart beating furiously. Poor little thing was terrified.

"The money," the man said again.

I reached out and he snatched the bills, clip and all, from my fingertips.

"Don't ever tell me how to run my business again," he snarled, and slammed the door in my face.

"There's not gonna be a next time, asshole," I said, and thanked the gods that the door had closed and left most of the stench inside where it belonged.

CHAPTER FOUR

The aroma was entirely much more pleasant when I opened the front door, stepped into my own house, and happily announced, "Honey! I'm home."

"You don't have to say that every time you walk through that door," Marina said, coming around the corner and planting a warm kiss on my lips.

"I know," I told her. "But I like to." I sniffed. "Is that what I think? Are we having your famous homemade tortilla soup for dinner?"

Marina cuddled up to me, putting her arms around my back and pressing her head to my chest. "Sorry, no," she said. "It's take-out from Casa de Soria." She looked up at me with sad eyes. "Are you disappointed?"

"I am not," I said. But I was. Casa de Soria was good, but nothing beat Marina's homemade tortilla soup.

Marina released me and padded into the front room. She was still wearing her work clothes, but she'd taken off her shoes and placed them neatly by the door. "I hear you had an interesting day," she said.

"Ah, you spoke to Melissa, I see."

"Yes," Marina said. "She said you rescued her dog from evil kidnappers."

"Evil assholes is a better word for them," I said. "And it cost her two hundred dollars."

"You couldn't talk them out of it?"

"Could have," I said. "Melissa wouldn't let me. Didn't want anybody to get hurt. Especially the dog."

Marina was almost done setting out the food. I could see a plate of enchiladas, another of refried beans and rice, and Marina's favorite, the chicken soft taco.

There were also a pair of golden margaritas, the salt rim shining like a run of diamonds.

Life was good.

After dinner, Marina and I sat in front of the TV, trying to find something to stream. There were so many networks and so many channels and so much to watch that it took us nearly as long to find a show as to watch it.

We finally settled on a new series starring Nicole Kidman and settled back. Nicole had just discovered that her husband had probably murdered someone when I drifted off.

CHAPTER FIVE

My office hours were posted in gold lettering on the frosted window of my office door. 8am-5pm. Couldn't be clearer. But I was still surprised when I rolled up at 8:27 to find two men sitting on the bench in the hallway waiting for me.

"Heller?" asked the smaller of the two men, standing. He was a couple of inches shorter than me and one of those guys who spends a good deal of his morning sprucing up. He was freshly and expertly shaved, and his hair was immaculately groomed—it fit the size and shape of his head perfectly. He wore what looked like an expensive suit, no tie, with a black t-shirt underneath. His feet were clad in what I assumed were ridiculously expensive sneakers, probably Gucci or Air Jordan.

I wasn't sure I liked the eager expression on his face.

"Yeah," I said. "Sorry I'm late. Had to stop for a Coke Zero."

"Coke Zero?" the first man said. "A man after my own heart. Never could stand coffee but people are always trying to force it on you."

"Would've brought you one if I'd known." I inserted the key in the lock, opened the door and used my open arm to welcome them in.

The first man gave me a nearly delirious smile as he squeezed past me and entered the office. The second man not so much. He gave me a dismissive glance through his impenetrable Ray-Ban sunglasses, and I realized he was there purely as muscle … and considered me no threat. He stood a good three inches over me, and he had the shoulders and barrel chest of a weightlifter. He, too, wore what looked like a ridiculously expensive suit but he wasn't gauche enough—or hip enough—to wear a t-shirt beneath. Instead, he wore a crisp, brilliantly white button up and a simple black tie knotted neatly around his muscle-swollen throat.

We pushed through the waiting room into my office, and I indicated the two client chairs in front of the desk. Instead of sitting, however, the smaller man walked over to stare at a framed newspaper clipping on the wall. The big man stood to the right of the door, clasped his hands in front of his abdomen, and stood at attention.

Who were these guys?

The smaller man chuckled. "The Shorts & Sandals Detective," he said after a moment. The clipping he'd been staring at was the first page of the Los Angeles Times story they'd done on me about four years ago.

Considering the shorts and sandals I was wearing, there was no denying it. "Yeah," I said. "Apparently, that's me."

"Kinda cool you kept the clipping," the man said. He turned away from the wall and took the client chair on my left. The larger man kept his post near the door.

"Wasn't my idea," I said. "The wife insisted. She cut it out, had it framed. If it was up to me, it wouldn't be there."

The man gave me a questioning look. "I didn't think you were married," he said.

I frowned. "Well, we're not. Don't even live together. It's just easier to explain that way." I gave him a look. "Not that's it's really any of your business."

He nodded.

"Listen, gentlemen, I'm at a disadvantage here. You obviously know a little about me, but who the hell are you?"

The smaller man leaned forward in the chair and nodded his head energetically. "Shale Monroe, producer. You've probably heard of me." Beaming, he extended his hand across the desk. I took it, gave it a quick shake.

Shale Monroe. The name was familiar, but I wasn't ready to admit it. I shook my head.

"Yeah, yeah, you've heard of me," Monroe insisted, waving away my uncertainty. "I've made a lot of big movies. *The Harder They Fall, Sunrunner, Day of the Falcon.* You've seen 'em, right?"

I nodded. I had seen them. All of them. And, worse, I *liked* them.

"Yeah, well, that's me," Monroe said. "I produced them. And a bunch more like them." He grinned. "And," he added, "I own the option to *that*!"

And he pointed at the framed clipping of the L.A. Times article on my wall.

"Oh," I said. "You're *that* guy."

"That's right, that's right," Monroe said. "And the good news is that we've decided to exercise our option. That puts twenty Gs in your pocket like now." He snapped his fingers to show me what "now" meant.

I realized that this was the day I had been dreading. Ever since some production company optioned the rights to the Los Angeles Times' Shorts and Sandals Detective article, I knew that the day might come when some idiot decided it would make a great movie. I'd signed my soul away, eager for a few easy bucks, and then I hoped and prayed The Shorts and Sandals Detective movie never made it to theaters. Or Netflix. Or anywhere.

But here I was now, the trigger had been pulled, and all I could get out of it was more money.

"Sure," I said. "I'll take twenty G's." I glanced over at the big man by the door, couldn't see his eyes through the dark lenses of his sunglasses. He could have been asleep. Standing, like a horse.

"Figured you would, my man, figured you would. Where do I send the check?" Shale asked.

"Same place as last time," I said. "My attorney ..."

"Robert Kaplan!" Monroe gushed. "Love me some Bobby."

Bobby wouldn't like being called that, I thought.

"Okay, we'll get that check cut. Mongo! Call Darlene. Tell her to cut that check and Fed Ex it to my man here."

"To Robert Kaplan," I said.

"To Bobby. Have her send it to Bobby."

Mongo pulled a cellphone out of his pocket and started texting.

"His name is Mongo?" I asked.

"Yeah, like in *Blazing Saddles*. That's not his real name, man, that's just what I call him. It's my pet name for him. His real name is Jonathan. Can you believe that? Jonathan. Takes too long to say. 'Jonathan, come here! There's a man with a gun!' See what I mean. It's so much easier to just say 'Mongo! I need you!'"

"Makes perfect sense to me." I took a sip of my Coke Zero, leaned back in my chair, "Well, it's a pleasure doing business with you, gentlemen, but—as I said—I have a busy morning."

"Well," Monroe said, leaning forward again and this time looking just the slightest bit sheepish. "There is *one* more thing."

There always is.

"Oh?" I said. "And what might that be?"

"Well, it's this: I'm going to be working on this script myself, Brace. I mean, I'm not writing it alone—we got a real writer to do the heavy lifting—but I'm going to be seriously involved and I'm taking screen credit, you bet your ass."

"As you should," I said.

"So, I wanna know what it's like to be a detective," Monroe said. "The Shorts and Sandals Detective. I wanna walk in your shoes. I wanna ride in your car. I wanna sleep in your bed."

43

"I can tell you at least two of those things aren't gonna happen."

"I don't mean literally," Monroe laughed. "I got my own shoes." He held up a foot to prove it to me. "I'm saying that I want to shadow you, observe you in action. Get an idea about who the *real* Shorts and Sandals Detective really is. You know, so I can incorporate it into my screenplay. Build the character. You know?"

I gave Monroe a disappointed smile. "Well, we can't do that," I said. "I'm a private detective. Accent on the *private*. I can't have some green-behind-the-ears movie producer and his mountain of a man security guard tagging along as I work."

"No, no, no," Monroe protested. "Mongo won't be there. Just me. He's only here in case I need something. But when it comes to the day-to-day stuff, it'll just be me."

I shook my head again. "Sorry," I said. "But that's not how I work. If that means it costs me $20,000, then so be it. I just can't do that."

Monroe gave me a sad smile. "I'm afraid you really don't have a choice."

I smirked. "Oh? I don't?"

"You've already signed off on it." Monroe reached back toward Mongo and the big man reached into his coat, withdrew a stack of stapled papers, and slapped them into his hand. Monroe tossed it on my desk.

I could read the words OPTION/PURCHASE AGREEMENT without even picking it up.

"It's there, highlighted on pages 2 and 3, under 'Miscellaneous.' If we exercise our option, you agree to a fourteen-day shadowing by our screenwriters." He smiled brightly. "And that's me!"

I read through the highlighted paragraph and felt my gut go cold. "Give me a minute," I said to Monroe.

"Take all the time you need."

I stepped out of my office, pulled out my cell phone and called my attorney, Robert Kaplan.

"Bobby!" I said, when he answered.

"Who the fuck is this?"

"It's your very favorite client," I told him.

"Brace Heller," he said, sighing. "You got some new band to sign or something?"

"Not yet, but I'm working on it," I said. "What I do have is Shale Monroe sitting in my office."

"Shale Monroe the producer?"

"I don't know anyone else named Shale."

"Good point. What's he doing there?"

"Well, he came to me with good news. He says he's going to exercise the option on The Shorts and Sandals Detective article and make a movie about me."

"Oh," Kaplan said. "Well, that *is* good news. What's your cut on that? It's like twenty grand, isn't it?"

"That's exactly what it is."

"So, you should be happy. Twenty grand just fell out of the skies and into your lap and you don't have to do anything but sit back and count the money."

"Don't I?"

"What do you mean?"

"I mean that Monroe thinks he has the right to shadow me for a week or two. Doing research for the movie or something."

"Why does he need to do that? He's a producer, not a writer."

"He says he's going to write it."

Kaplan snorted. "Everyone thinks they're a writer," he said.

"So I have to do it?"

"Is it in the agreement?"

"You wrote the goddamn thing!"

"You think I memorized it? Is it in the agreement?"

"This is what it says," I told him, and read him the highlighted text.

"Yeah, you're going to have to do it," he said.

"How am I supposed to do that? I'm a private detective. People expect me to take care of their *private* business. How am I supposed to do anything private when I have a goddamn movie producer peering over my shoulders?"

"He's going to have to sign an NDA."

"A what?"

"An NDA. A Non-Disclosure Agreement. He's going to have to sign one for every client who hires you during the time he's here. And you're going to have to get permission from each one of them."

"Fuck me."

"I'll write one up and get it over to you," Kaplan said. "Hey, look at it this way. You're getting twenty thousand dollars for two weeks' work. That's way more than your usual fee."

I stepped back into the office and pushed the OPTION/PURCHASE AGREEMENT back into Monroe's hands. Kaplan had a copy if I needed one. I sat down behind my desk, opened the lower right drawer, and pulled out three plastic shot glasses and a bottle of Maker's Mark.

"Gentlemen," I said. "It seems that we have an agreement."

CHAPTER SIX

When I got home that evening, I found a crock pot full of Marina's homemade tortilla soup simmering in the kitchen, its savory aroma filling every corner of the room with homey comfort. There was also a note from Marina. She said that her mother was sick and that she'd gone to L.A. to be with her. She signed it with her usual M and an effusive heart, promising she'd be back the next day.

I took a quick hot shower, slipped on a pair of basketball shorts, and went back into the kitchen. My mouth watered as the glass lid came off the crock pot and a wave of pure olfactory pleasure overwhelmed me. I spooned out a giant bowl, grabbed a bag of tortilla chips and Mrs. Renfro

Salsa, and retired to the front room. Wurzel followed hope-fully, his energy level shooting up at the prospect of maybe getting a bite of chicken.

I ate my soup and drank a Lagunitas IPA and watched ancient television shows that I barely remembered as a kid. Currently, it was *Voyage to the Bottom of the Sea* with Richard Basehart and David Hedison. The episode I was watching was about a werewolf on an island with a radioactive vol-cano. High art, indeed. I loved every minute of it.

I finished my first bowl of soup and then scooped out another, returning to the La-Z-Boy for more adventures in the *Seaview*. At some point, Wurzel finally got the piece of chicken he was so vibrantly hoping for.

The credit "Produced by Irwin Allen" flashed across the screen and Shale Monroe came to mind. I'd seen his movies. I'd liked his movies. I wasn't exactly sure what a movie producer did, but Monroe seemed to know how to do it well. He'd certainly been successful enough.

And he didn't seem to be a bad guy. A little wired, per-haps. Energetic might be a better word. But he'd been dip-lomatic and pleasant enough at the office today, even if he had never intended to take no for an answer. He wasn't one of those Hollywood blowhards who thought they could solve every problem simply by throwing money at it.

Of course, he had thrown $20,000 at me and that had pretty much solved his problem today.

The first real test would come tomorrow morning. I had an appointment with a potential client at 8:00 AM and told Monroe to meet me at the office twenty minutes prior. We had to run through the NDA that Kaplan wrote up, and he had to sign it or there was no deal, twenty grand or not. And the client had to sign off on it, too, and there was no guarantee that was going to happen either.

Regardless, it would be an interesting couple of weeks.

An idea popped into my head. According to the clock on the wall, it was just about 9:30. Too late to call Ritchie the Bean but the hell with it. I was up. The least he could do was take my call.

I paused Netflix and grabbed my cell and punched in Ritchie's number. The phone rang once and then quickly went to voicemail. Too quickly. He was avoiding my call. I immediately called again. Same result. I called a third time and finally Ritchie picked up the phone.

"Okay, okay!" he said. "What's so goddamn important?"

Ritchie the Bean was a film producer and minor crime kingpin who lived in the hills of Santa Paula. Ritchie had made most of his money from a run of films his grandfather had produced in the 60s, living off them ever since, and dabbling in the criminal element at the same time. He'd been able to cut down on the crime angle of his business recently, due to the comeback success of his franchise films, *Wolverine Sisters*, on Netflix. Ritchie owned and licensed his grandfather's library around the world and had produced thirty-one films himself. I figured if anybody knew anything about Shale Monroe, Ritchie was the guy.

"Ritchie, it's Heller," I said.

"I know that, goddammit," Ritchie spat. "It says that on the goddamn phone!"

"I didn't wake you, did I?"

"Of course, you fucking woke me," Ritchie said. "It's the middle of the goddamn night!"

"Ritchie, it's not even ten o'clock."

"Middle of the goddamn night," Ritchie groused. "What the hell do you want, Brace?"

"I need some information," I said. "On a film producer. Figured you might know him."

"What's his name?" From the way Ritchie was slurring his words, I was certain he'd used a series of Mojitos as sleep aids yet again.

"Shale Monroe," I said. *Day of the Falcon*. You know him?"

"Shale Monroe," Ritchie repeated. "What the hell you doing with him?"

"Apparently, he owns the option to that article the Times did about me. You know, The Shorts and Sandals Detective."

Ritchie laughed. "That's so goddamn funny," he said. "The Shorts and Sandals Detective." He snorted. "Hey, why'd you sell the rights to him? You coulda sold 'em to me. We're pals, remember? I shoulda got first dibs."

"I didn't sell them to anybody, Ritchie. The Times did. I just got roped into the deal."

"Shoulda sold 'em to me."

"Anyway, Monroe's in town, shadowing me for research or something. I just wondered what you could tell me about him. Wondered if you knew him."

"Everyone knows Shale," Ritchie said. "He's one of those young bucks who thinks a producer's supposed to be as big a star as his leads. Always got a hot dame at his elbow, always showing up at parties. *Entertainment Tonight* probably has footage of him riding a goddamn zipline in Argentina."

"Yeah," I said. "I've seen him on those shows. A lot."

"Camera loves him," Ritchie said. "And he's good for business, too. When a Shale Monroe picture comes out, you know it. And usually directly from Shale."

"What do you know about him?" I asked. "Is he a good guy?"

"Fuck, no, he's not a good guy," Ritchie spat. "He's a Hollywood Producer for chrissake. None of us are good guys. But he knows what he's doing, you know? He knows how to take a rinky-dink screenplay and turn it into a billion-dollar film franchise. He's good at that, I can tell ya."

"Do you think it's safe to let him hang for a couple of weeks?"

"Didn't I just say 'fuck, no?'" Ritchie said. "But you probably don't have any choice, am I right? Contract got one of those 'observation' clauses in it?"

"Yeah."

"Well, then you're stuck. But I will say there are worse guys you could be stuck with. Coppola for one. Fucking prick. Thinks he's too good for *Wolverine Sisters 4*."

"Ritchie, as always, you're a wealth of information," I said. "Thanks for taking my call. Now go back to sleep."

"Seriously, Brace, you should have sold the rights to me," Ritchie said, his sleepy voice fading out just like a movie.

The call cut off. I stared at the screen for a moment and smiled.

There was a spoonful of soup still in my bowl, so I tilted it back and drank it down. Wurzel whined anxiously but there was no soup for him. I turned off *Voyage to the Bottom of the Sea*, rinsed out my bowl in the sink and told Wurzel it was time for bed.

I read about twenty pages of the latest Peter Ash novel, marked it with a business card, turned off the light and fell asleep to the sounds of Wurzel's soft rolling snore beside me.

CHAPTER SEVEN

Monroe was there on time, looking bright-eyed and bushy-tailed. He and Mongo sat on the bench outside of my office, and Monroe jumped to his feet as I came toward them down the hall. I gave Monroe one of the two large Coke Zero's I'd purchased at Chick Fil A on the way in. He gave me what looked like a genuine smile of thanks.

"'sup, Mongo," I said to the big man.

Instead of returning the greeting, he gave a low, rumbling growl from deep within his throat as he stood. He made a point of looking down at me, making sure I was aware of the height difference, and then looked away.

He was like Lurch of the Addams Family in Dave Bautista's body.

"I'll text you when we're done," Monroe said to Mongo, as I opened the office door. "Call me if anything important comes up."

Mongo gave another one of those brief growls and left us standing in the hall.

Monroe had changed his clothes since we last parted and it felt a little weird to me. He was wearing cargo shorts, a Twisted Sister t-shirt, and a pair of Teva sandals.

"Nice shirt," I said. "Where'd you get it?"

"eBay," he said. "Fifty bucks."

"Fifty bucks!" I yelped. "That shirt's gotta be thirty years old."

"It's not old," Monroe told me. "It's *vintage*."

We sat at my desk, and he looked over the NDA and then signed it with a Hollywood flourish. I was certain his armada of lawyers had vetted it before he even thought about putting pen to paper. "Now what?" he asked.

"Now we wait for our client," I said. The clock on the wall said it was two minutes to eight. "But first we're gonna cover a couple of ground rules: Rule #1 – you sit over there in the corner, away from the desk. Rule #2 – I do all the talking. You're here to observe, not take part. Rule #3 – NDA or no NDA, if I found out you've talked about the people we see here in the next couple weeks, I will take it as a personal affront. And there will be consequences."

Monroe waved any concern away. "I get it, I get it," he said. "But I do have one question."

"Which is?"

"When do I get my piece?"

My jaw dropped open in what must have been comical astonishment. Monroe laughed and pointed at me. "I'm just shittin' you, man," he said. "You should have seen your face."

"Over there," I said, pointing to the chair in the corner.

"I'm going, I'm going."

He walked away from the desk and took his seat in the corner near the coat rack. I glanced at the clock, 8:01, and back at Monroe. He grinned widely and shot me with his thumb and forefinger.

"So, what do you think the case is gonna be?"

"The case?" I asked. "What are you? Perry Mason?"

"You know what I mean."

"Most of the time, it's a cheating spouse," I said. "Sometimes, it's finding a lost person. Lawyers sometimes ask me to do observation work for them. Get photos of a guy on disability who's moving a refrigerator into his house. I do a little corporate work, too. Catch employees stealing office machines, cheating on their timesheets, that kind of stuff."

"How often is it murder?"

"Not very often," I said. "That's where the police come in."

We heard a click and the waiting room door swung open. The silhouette of a man shimmered in the reeded glass that separated the waiting room from the front office. Our client had arrived. I stood, opened the office door, and peered out.

"Mr. Wilder?"

"Yes. And you're Mr. Heller?"

"Brace," I said. "Yes. Please come in."

I stood back and let Wilder pass me as he came through the office door. He was a reedy little man, at least six inches shorter than me, and he dressed like one of the nerds from

IT. He wore a pair of khaki trousers, a white button up shirt, and black shoes shined somewhere between too glossy and not glossy enough.

A single pen was stuck in his left front pocket. At least he didn't have the full pocket protector there.

"Mr. Wilder, this is my associate ..." the word stuck in my throat like a Goo Goo Cluster, and I had to force it out through my lips. "... Mr. Shale Monroe."

Monroe rose from his corner and approached Wilder with his hand out as though they'd met at a party just the night before. They shook. "Pleased to meet you, Mr. Wilder. Thanks for coming in." Monroe released the man's hand and gave him one of his stunning Hollywood smiles.

There was a reason Monroe was one of those producers who was almost as popular as the movie stars in his films.

"Nice to meet you," Wilder said meekly. He turned his attention to me. "I'm sorry, Mr. Heller. I didn't expect an associate."

"Honestly, neither did I," I said. "Mr. Monroe is a film producer who's doing research on a character for one of his films."

Wilder's eyes widened slightly.

"He's shadowing me for the next couple of weeks to get some background for the screenplay to his next film."

"How interesting," Wilder said, glancing back at Monroe, who shot him a gleeful thumbs up.

"I know this is awkward and unexpected," I said. "But I want you to know that I only agreed to this with the understanding that Mr. Monroe is here only to observe. He is forbidden to talk about anything he witnesses here under penalty of law."

I lowered my hand and offered Wilder the client chair. "Of course, the choice is entirely yours," I continued. "If this makes you uncomfortable and you'd prefer not to talk in front of Mr. Monroe, we can make other arrangements."

I saw Monroe stiffen behind me. We hadn't discussed that option.

Wilder took a deep breath through his nose and cast one more cautious look in Monroe's direction. "How do I know he won't say anything?" he asked. "End up using my misfortune in one of his films?"

"Because he signed a Non-Disclosure Agreement," I said, picking the paper off the desk and offering it to Wilder. "If he does, we sue his ass. And, trust me, he's got really deep pockets."

Wilder gave a little smile at that. He read quickly through the NDA and then nodded. "I guess I'm okay with it," he said, and sat down.

I went back around the desk and sat down on my side. "Tell me what brings you here, Mr. Wilder," I said.

"Please call me Dylan," Wilder said. "And it's my wife. I think she's having an affair."

"What's your wife's name?"

"Kathy," Wilder said. "Katherine."

"With a K?"

"Yes."

I made a quick note and shot Monroe a glance that Wilder didn't see. "What makes you think that?"

"She's been distant lately. Aloof," Wilder said. "Staying late at the office; staying too long at the Club."

"Club? What Club?"

"The Lemon Grove Racquet Club," Wilder told me. "Out there in …"

"Saticoy," I said. "Yes, I know."

"We're members and she's been going there virtually every single day for lunch for, I don't know, ten years. But it was just lunch. Now, she stays later, sometimes an hour or two later after the dining room closes. I don't know what she's doing, but she sure isn't coming home."

"How's it been at home?" I asked.

"Like I said, quiet. Aloof. She doesn't seem to want to talk much anymore. We used to talk about my day, about her day, stuff like that. But we don't do that anymore. We come home, we eat dinner, we watch TV, we go to bed. Separately. I'm usually in bed before she is."

"How's the sex?" Monroe asked from his corner. I shot him an angry look. But really, that would have been my next question, too.

"What?" Wilder said. They always said that. Gave them time to think.

"My associate ..." the word caught in my throat again, a tarantula crawling down my esophagus. "... is asking a valid question."

Wilder shook his head. "It's ... it's all right," he said. "I mean, we don't do it as often as we used to, but who does?"

I pretended to make a quick note. "Any strange calls? Late at night? Hang-ups?"

Wilder's eyes opened. "Why, yes," he said. "I've heard a couple of those but didn't think anything about them. You know. Telemarketers."

"Sure."

"Is that a bad sign?"

"Could be."

"I didn't even think about that," Wilder said softly.

"If you'd like us to, we'll take your case, Mr. Wilder," I said. "I'm not sure you need us. Your wife may not be having an affair. She might just be tired. But I understand that sometimes it feels better to know for sure that there is nothing going on." I frowned. "Or, that there is."

"Yes, I agree," Wilder said, reaching into his back pocket and producing a checkbook. "How does this work?"

I gave him my rates and he hesitantly wrote out a check. That was normal. They wrote the check slowly, debating with themselves whether it was worth the money or not. They almost always decided it was.

Wilder tore off a check and handed it to me. "When will you start?" he asked.

"First thing tomorrow," I said.

"What will you do?"

"Leave that up to me. Better you don't know. Did you bring a photo of your wife?"

"Yes." He reached into his shirt pocket, retrieved a snapshot, and passed it over to me. I gave it a quick glance. Mrs. Wilder was an attractive woman. Fit. Sun-tanned. Well-dressed.

"And the information form?"

"Yes," He took a folded paper from the same pocket the photo came from and slid it over to me. I opened it and gave it the once-over. Seemed like everything was filled out. Name. Address. Phone number. Employer. All the usual 411.

"Thanks," I said. "Give me a few days and I'll be in touch. We'll talk about what we've discovered."

"Thank you," Wilder said and, for a second, I felt that he was on the verge of tears. This was another typical reaction. I knew that this was the point where everyone had second thoughts. It wasn't about the money this time. It was about a sense of betrayal. Guilt over hiring a private investigator to spy on the person they loved most in the world.

"Thank you," Wilder said again, more softly this time. He stood and walked calmly out of the office, carefully closing the door behind him as he stepped out into the hallway.

Monroe stood and clapped his hands together eagerly, the resounding crack startling me. "So!" he said. "Let's go catch this bitch!"

"Sit the hell back down," I said sharply, pointing my finger at him.

Monroe gave me a surprised, hurt look.

"You need to understand something," I told him. "This isn't one of your movies. It's not one of your screenplays. If we find out that woman is cheating on her husband, we will ruin both of their lives. It's not an adventure. It's real life and sometimes, it sucks. Chances are that she's just tired, or bored, and is hanging out with her gal pals at the Club. Chances are she's never cheated on her husband, despite the fact he's obviously so boring."

"I'm sorry," Monroe mumbled. "I didn't realize …"

"Well, you do now," I said. "This is a job. Like most jobs sometimes it really blows. So, let's hope we find out this woman just discovered how much she enjoys billiards and has been spending time practicing and not hiding out in the sauna blowing the pool boy."

Monroe looked at me meekly. "I don't think they have billiards at a place called the Lemon Grove Racquet Club," he said.

I tried not to but laughed anyway. "Shut up, asshole," I said.

CHAPTER EIGHT

I was just about to introduce Monroe to the wonderful world of Google (the private detective's best friend) when my cell rang. It was Marina. I thumbed the answer slide but before I could even say hello, I knew something was wrong.

"Brace," Marina said, the moment the call connected. "My mom died."

The words hit me like a fist to the gut. I knew that Marina's mother had been ill, but I thought it was just a cold or, at worst, the flu. "Oh, my God, honey," was all I could manage. It felt weak, insufficient.

"She had ... she had that flu, you know," Marina went on. "And it didn't get better, so I came down. I thought I could help her get better. But she just kept getting worse."

Monroe waved his hand to get my attention and then signed that he was excusing himself. He stepped out of my office, walked through the waiting room, and entered the hallway.

"Baby, I'm so sorry," I said. "When did this happen?" I couldn't bring myself to say *When did she die?*

"About an hour ago, maybe more," Marina said, sniffling. She was the strongest woman I had ever known, and she was powering through this, but the edges were showing. "We were at the house, and she suddenly got really bad, coughing, and throwing up. Her fever spiked so we rushed her to the hospital. They took her in right away but then they told us ..." She took a second to catch her breath. "They told us she had a stroke."

"A stroke?"

"Yes, they said that sometimes after someone is sick with the flu that their chances of having a stroke go way up." Another deep breath and then a whisper: "Oh, mommy."

"I'm so sorry, Marina," I said, feeling inadequate once again. "I'm on my way. I can be there in an hour."

I heard her take a few deep breaths as she tried to settle herself. "No, honey," she said after a moment. "Don't. There's nothing you can do. Anyway, someone's got to take care of Wurzel. And somebody has to water my plants."

"I can find somebody to do that," I said.

"No, please don't," Marina said. "Just feed that fat Boston of yours and make sure my plants don't die." Her voice hitched on the word. "I need you there, for now. I'll call you in a couple of days and let you know when the service is. You can come down then."

"I want to be there," I said.

"I know you do, but it's better this way," Marina said. "You know my family. I'm going to be so busy getting them settled. Give me a day or two just to get things done."

"I can help you get things done."

"Brace … please."

I sighed. "Okay. But please promise me you'll call me the moment you need something."

"I will, honey," Marina said.

"You okay?"

"No."

"I know."

"I love you."

"I love you, too."

The call ended.

I sat back in my office chair and thought about Esmeralda Espinoza. We'd first met just four or five years ago, right after I'd started dating her daughter. Marina told me to beware of her mother, that she was a charming woman on the outside but a cunning spy on the inside. She told me that I wouldn't have any secrets after ten minutes chatting with her mother, and she wasn't far wrong.

Esmeralda was one of those people who could make it seem as though you were having a perfectly common conversation with her—even if half of that conversation was in Spanish—but immediately after that conversation you stopped and thought about what you'd talked about, and you realized that you'd given up a lot more than she had.

But Esmeralda didn't do that because she was the cunning spy that Marina was talking about. Esmeralda did that because she loved people. She loved to learn about them, find out what made them tick, to make them reveal what they loved.

And if she uncovered something she didn't like, she didn't judge. She just made a mental note not to bring up that particular subject ever again.

I leaned back in my chair and tried to imagine that bubbly, cheerful woman lying still in a hospital bed sixty miles away and I couldn't do it. Esmeralda had been all about life. It seemed impossible that death had taken her.

Monroe popped his head back in. "Everything all right?" he asked.

"That would be a no," I said. "My wife's mother died."

"Jesus Christ. I'm sorry, man. Jesus."

I nodded.

"How'd she die?"

"Stroke."

"She here in town?"

"No," I said. "She lived in Los Angeles. Marina is down there with her now."

"You heading down?"

I shook my head. "Not yet," I said. "Marina asked me not to. In a couple of days."

Monroe gave me a quizzical look.

"She's Hispanic, you know? Mexican. So that means she's got a huge family. I mean aunts and uncles and cousins up the yin-yang. And they all loved her mother. They'll converge down there now, all of them. They're so close. It's what they do." I sighed. "I'm not kidding, there'll be literally hundreds of them. I'd just be in the way."

Monroe nodded as though he understood. Maybe he did.

"Let's call it a day," he said.

I gave him an appreciative look. "Thanks."

"See you tomorrow?"

"Tomorrow works."

"Call me if you need something."

And one of the world's biggest movie producers walked out of my office, leaving me with the thought that maybe he wasn't such a bad guy after all.

CHAPTER NINE

The atomic clock on the wall read 11:39a. It also told me
the temperature outside was 76.5 and it was Wednesday.
Monroe had been gone for over an hour.

I sat at my office desk with the lights off, leaned back
in my desk chair and sipped on a shot of Makers Mark. The
bottle sat on my desk, its red-waxed cap beside it, in case
another pour was required.

It just might be.

It wasn't that my mother-in-law and I were what you
would say *close*. I mean, we got along. We respected one
another. We had fun when we went out to dinner, and we
didn't end up screaming at each other about politics over
turkey or ham at Thanksgiving and Christmas.

But I was thinking about how much different and how much more difficult her death would be for Marina. How much of an impact it was going to make on her life. She and her mother were about as close as a mother and daughter could be. Daily phone call, without fail. Texting throughout the day as well (Marina had bought Esmeralda an iPhone and taught her how to use it for just that purpose). Their relationship had only intensified when Marina's father, Javier, had passed away four years earlier.

It was going to be brutal for her over the next few days. Making funeral arrangements, fielding phone calls from friends and family, writing and publishing the obituary. I knew she'd also be in charge of putting up the family members who were coming in out of town. Some would stay with brothers or sisters who lived in L.A. Others would need hotel rooms and they'd expect Marina to do the footwork. She knew which hotels were clean and safe to stay at. They didn't. They were out-of-towners.

I wanted nothing more than to be there with her. At least I could give her a helping hand. I could make hotel reservations just as easily as she could. I could deal with the funeral home and the newspaper. Most importantly, I could be there for emotional support.

But I knew where Marina was coming from. She preferred to do everything on her own because that way she knew it would be done right. She wouldn't have to worry about her Uncle Jorge bitching about his crappy hotel room. She wouldn't have to be concerned that the obituary offended anybody by leaving out a "survived by" name. She didn't have to keep her fingers crossed that someone chose the right caterer for the reception.

So, there I was, sitting there in my office, in the dark, pouring myself another finger of Makers Mark, when Puño walked in.

I've known Puño most of my adult life and it still amazed me to watch him move. He was six feet, five inches of solid muscle and moved like the proverbial big cat. To see him, you'd think he would be awkward and clumsy. That would be an assumption that would cost you later.

He came through the waiting room and pushed his way into my office. Swinging a leg over the client's chair, he grabbed the bottle of whiskey and poured a healthy amount into a coffee cup that I saved for clients. He took a sip, enjoyed it, and then looked at me.

"Sorry to hear about Marina's mom," he said. "She was a good lady."

I gave him a look. "And you know that how?" I asked. "I mean, you only met her … what? … once?"

"Once can be enough to know if someone is a good person or not," Puño said. He took another sip of whiskey. "She was a good person."

"She was," I agreed. "How'd you find out?"

"Marina texted me," Puño told me. "Asked me to come down in a few days for the service."

"Yeah, that's what she told me, too."

"Wants us to stay out of her way."

"That's the way she does things."

"I felt bad. Told her I can't make it," Puño said. "I'll be in Mexico most of next week."

"What are you doing in Mexico?" I asked.

"Getting my truck upholstered."

"Ah," I said. "Of course."

We sat and sipped whiskey for a while and it felt good.

"Need a favor," Puño said.

"Ah," I replied. "The truth rises."

"You remember my ex, Cassandra?"

"Sure."

"She's seeing this new guy. Name of Locke. Locke Reynolds."

"Locke? Like Master Lock?"

"No," Puño said. "Got an 'e' at the end."

"Wouldn't that be Lock-ee?" I teased.

"It would not."

"Okay," I said. "And?"

"And I don't like him."

"Because his name is Locke?"

"One reason," Puño said. "Got some others."

I smirked. "You two thinking about getting back together?"

"With Cassandra!" Puño exclaimed. "No fuckin' way. That bitch is crazy!"

"Okay, so why don't you like him, this Locke guy?"

Puño emptied his coffee cup and pushed it over for more. I filled it maybe a quarter of the way, was sad to see the bottle was almost empty. "See, so I ran into Cassandra yesterday," Puño said.

"Oh? How is she?"

"She's fine except for the pair of black eyes she got, plus the bruises on her arm."

I nodded. "That's why you don't like the guy."

"I asked her, what's up with all the bruises? She says she fell down the stairs at work."

"Maybe she did."

"She forgot. I know where she works. Ain't no stairs there to fall down."

"Oh," I said. "Shit."

"Yeah, shit," Puño said. "Here's the thing. Maybe she did fall down or something. Hurt herself. And she's embarrassed to say how."

"Maybe."

"I mean, I've done it. Missed a step, fell down some stairs. Kicked a curb, lost my balance. Cracked my head on an open cupboard door."

"We all have."

"Point is, I don't want him putting hands on her."

"If he is."

"If he is." Puño tipped the coffee cup, drank some whiskey. "And I gotta find out. Thing is, I shouldn't be the one to find out."

"A little biased?"

Puño nodded. "Might see some things that aren't there."

"So, you want me to find out."

"Would you?"

"So you don't mistake a gentle love tap for a smack to the face?"

"That's right."

"Because this new beau is going to be in some serious trouble if he's beating your ex-wife."

Puño thought about that a moment. "Doesn't really matter if it's my ex-wife or somebody else's ex-wife," he said. "Shit shouldn't be happening."

"Understood," I said. "We should probably discuss my rates."

"Fuck your rates."

I understood that, too.

CHAPTER TEN

I showed up at the office at the time posted on the door (for once), 8:00 AM, with a cardboard Jack-in-the-Box drink holder containing two large Coke Zero's. They were stupid expensive but were usually pretty good and I had a feeling that Shale Monroe would be on time.

He was. Sitting on the bench in the hallway outside my office with Mongo right beside him. As I approached, Mongo stood and walked away without saying a word. I tried not to show how much that hurt me and turned my focus to Monroe.

"Morning," I told him.

"Morning," he said, standing. "How are things?"

I gave him the sodas and used my key to open the door. We went inside and took our places in the inner office.

"I talked to Marina last night," I told him after we'd settled. "She says things are going as well as can be, considering."

"Well, that's something."

"I'll be heading down there Tuesday so Tuesday and Wednesday will have to be off days for us. I should be back on Thursday morning."

"Not a problem. I understand completely."

"What have you two been up to?" I asked as I powered up the computer.

"Trying out the local restaurants," Monroe said. "Me and Mongo. So far, my favorite is the Aloha Steakhouse, down by the pier?" I nodded that I knew it. "But we had a blast at Barrelhouse, across the street."

"Barrelhouse 101."

"Yeah, that's it. Tons of beer and some amazing pub food."

"Good. There's a lot of great places out there."

Monroe laughed. "I'll keep hunting them down."

"Bring your chair over here," I said, adjusting the monitor so it could be seen by both of us. "Here's your first lesson."

"On the computer?" Shale asked, sliding his chair next to mine.

"You'd be surprised how much detective work is done with search engines," I told him. "I always start with Google because they're the biggest and the most extensive. But there's also Yahoo, Bing and at least a dozen of others you haven't heard of."

I typed "Dylan Wilder" in the search bar. Monroe gave me a questioning look.

"I always start with the client," I told him. "Want to make sure they're who they say they are. I've had a couple of assholes walk in here who turned out to be stalkers, wanting me to do their dirty work. Screw them."

"No shit," Monroe said absently.

I hit the ENTER key and the screen switched to a list.

Monroe whistled. "Almost thirty thousand hits."

"Yeah, we've got to narrow it down," I said. "But first, let's look at this."

I clicked a link that read JOSEPH WILDER PRO-FILES | FACEBOOK and the browser took us there. A list of about six possibilities appeared, complete with photos and locations.

"See anybody you recognize?" I asked.

"There he is," Monroe said, pointing at the fifth link.

"That's our guy," I said. "And it tells us that, doesn't it?" I read from the screen. "Joseph Wilder. CPA. Lives in Ventura, California." I clicked on the link, and it took us to Wilder's Facebook page. "And, if you're logged into Facebook," I told Monroe, "You can browse their page."

Sure enough, Wilder's Facebook page appeared. The banner was a photo of an ancient abacus, and the profile picture was our client as he appeared probably five or six years ago.

"You can find out where he went to high school," I continued, using the cursor as a laser pointer, "You can find out if he's in a relationship." Wilder's profile proclaimed *Married to Kathy Wilder*. "You can find out where they went for vacation." There were multiple photos filled with palm trees, slate blue seas, and fiery orange sunsets.

"Hawaii," I said, and pointed to a photo of the Grand Hyatt Kauai Resort & Spa.

"You'll also notice in this photo of Mr. and Mrs. Wilder," I said, touching the screen, "that the person sitting beside our friend Dylan is the same woman in the photo he gave us this morning. Our objective, Mrs. Katherine Wilder."

Monroe leaned forward for a better look. He glanced from the screen to the photo on my desktop. "Identification confirmed," he said.

"It would seem that way," I agreed. "But we've got a lot more research to do."

We spent the rest of the afternoon gathering what information we could. We found Mrs. Wilder's Facebook page—the banner photo, a gorgeous sunset in what was probably Kauai—and discovered that she belonged to a coffee klatch that met several times a week at the Lemon Grove Racquet Club. According to her profile, she was a retired salesperson, she enjoyed cooking and her favorite television show was *The Walking Dead* although she was glad it finally ended because she was getting tired of all those spin-offs.

Drapery World was her former employer, according to LinkedIn, and she collected cute dog videos on her YouTube page. According to Yelp, she was angry at her mechanic, saying that he failed to fix her ongoing air conditioning problem and neglected to return her calls about rectifying the problem. "How do you drive around with no air conditioning when you live in Ventura?" she had written and, so far, 31 people had found her comment USE-FUL, two found it FUNNY and one person had even marked it COOL, perhaps as a lame attempt at a pun.

It was beginning to get dark outside when we completed our profile at just after 5 o'clock. We now had a lot of information on Mrs. Katherine Wilder of Ventura, California. Most of it would probably be useless to us but some of it might be gold. Only time would tell.

"You want a beer?" I asked Monroe, indicating the tiny refrigerator in the corner.

He glanced at his watch. "Would love one, but I gotta go," he said. "Me and Mongo are checking out this Italian place, Café Fiore, tonight. You been there?"

"I have," I said. "Excellent."

"Good, good," Monroe said, standing. "Hey, you wanna come?"

I thought about it. A big plate of lasagna sounded pretty damn good. But I had work to do.

"Nah, you go ahead," I said. "Maybe next time."

"I'm buying," Monroe said.

I laughed. "Tempted, but I better pass. See you tomorrow."

"Okay, your loss," Monroe said, heading for the door. He opened it and then turned back to me. "What's the plan for tomorrow?" he asked.

"Tomorrow," I told him, "We visit the Lemon Grove Racquet Club."

CHAPTER ELEVEN

Cassandra Walker, Puño's ex-wife, lived in an aging single-family home on the west end of Ventura, on a street that was perpendicular to Ventura Avenue, the main drag, better known as "The Avenue" to locals. The neighborhood she lived in wasn't bad, but it wasn't particularly good, either. (A particularly bad neighborhood, however, was just around the corner.)

Cassandra's home wasn't rundown or filthy, but it was old and, for the most part, unkempt, at least from what I could see from my location. I was parked one house down, on the opposite side of the street, with a pair of binoculars and a bag of hot dogs from Der Wienerschnitzel on the passenger seat beside me.

The yard wasn't much of a yard anymore, pretty much just dirt and the occasional weed, and the driveway was cracked and crumbling. A yellow light burned through cozy curtains that bordered what I believed was the kitchen window. Cassandra's car, a 1980 Chevy Impala—the same car she'd owned when she was married to Puño—sat in the driveway, looking even worse for wear than the house's exterior paint.

The sun was sinking into the sea and the cool blue evening was just settling in. I loved this time of day. Everything seemed so much clearer, so much crisper. I don't know if it was just a trick of the light or if my eyes just worked better at this time of day, but it calmed me. Made me feel peaceful.

It was time for a hot dog.

I opened the Wienerschnitzel bag and withdrew one of the paper-wrapped dogs from within. Opening the wrapper, I discovered it was a mustard dog, one of my favorites, just about as simple a hot dog as you can get (unless you like them without any topping whatsoever). I took a bite and washed it down with a swig of Diet Pepsi.

The podcast app was open on my phone and I scanned through the directory trying to find something interesting. I finally settled on a Cold Cases show, this one about a murder in San Francisco that took place in 1975. Of course, the podcasters never actually came up with any realistic answers about the cold cases they discussed but they were still fun to listen to.

I had finished up my mustard dog and was halfway through the chili cheese dog when a pair of headlights indicated that a car had just turned onto the street. I waited until it passed me, then reluctantly put down the remains of my hot dog and picked up the binoculars.

The car wasn't a car after all but rather a beat-up Ford pick-up. From the looks of it, the truck was a workhorse. Somebody used it for construction work or plumbing. Sure enough, it turned into Cassandra's driveway and parked beside her Impala. I watched through binocular lenses as the person inside gathered some items in the cab and then stepped out.

The man who stepped out of the truck stood one or two inches beneath the top of the cab which, by my estimate, made him about 5' 10" or so. His work shirt was slung over his shoulder, leaving his shoulders bared in a yellowed sleeveless undershirt. A black tattoo of the old Punisher skull icon stared back at me from his bicep. The dirt and grime on the heavy-duty work pants he wore spoke volumes about the physicality of his job. The pair of battered boots on his feet seemed two sizes too big for the rest of his body. He juggled an equally battered polyester lunch bag and a stainless-steel coffee mug as he headed for the house.

It was Locke. He fit the description that Puño had given me, right down to the Punisher tattoo.

Locke disappeared from view as he headed toward the house, and I took that as my cue. I double-checked to make sure the dome light was off, opened the door and headed down my side of the sidewalk. As I drew directly across the street from the house, I kneeled and pretended to tie my shoe, straining my ears to catch any bits of conversation. There was only the sound of night insects and the distant hum of cars on Ventura Avenue. I got up and continued down the street to the next corner.

I crossed the street there and walked back up toward Cassandra's house. I stopped on the sidewalk directly opposite the lit window and pretended I was reading and replying to a text. The murmur of conversation from inside reached my ears but I couldn't make out a single word.

I finished my "text," and walked past the house and across the street to the Camry. I climbed back in, sadly looked down at my cold, coagulated chili cheese dog, and settled back.

It was going to be a long night.

At just after 11:00pm, the light in the kitchen winked out and the house went dark. I waited another twenty minutes and, when the only thing I could hear was a cat yowling in the night, I started up the Camry and U-Turned to head home.

CHAPTER TWELVE

FaceTiming wasn't the same as being there, but it was better than nothing.

It was almost midnight. I was in my living room in Ventura and Marina was in her mom's house 70 miles away. We were both staring at our iPhones, looking longingly at each other's images, and wishing we were together.

"How are you doing?" It was Marina, asking me. And she was the one whose mother had just died.

"I'm fine," I said. "Wish I was there with you, but otherwise fine." I sensed that she didn't want to talk about her mom, their family, or the impending service.

"I know," she said. "Tuesday."

"Yes. Tuesday."

"So, what'd you do tonight?" Marina asked. She was sipping what looked like Chardonnay from a stemless wineglass.

"I just got home," I told her. "Spent the evening eating chili cheese dogs and spying on Puño's ex-wife's house."

"What's that all about?"

"Puño asked me to keep an eye on her," I said. "Thinks she might be getting punched around by her new boyfriend."

"Fucker."

"Well, yes, if he's guilty. This is one of those times that you want to make 100% sure he's doing what he's accused of doing before you make any decisions."

"Because of what Puño will do."

"Because of Puño," I confirmed.

She drank a little of her wine. I sipped a little Makers Mark.

"What's on the agenda tomorrow?" Marina asked.

"We're going to the Lemon Grove Racquet Club."

Marina made a puzzled face. "Why? For lunch or something?"

"What? I don't strike you as the tennis type?"

"No," Marina said plainly. "You don't."

"Work," I said. "Potentially cheating spouse. Me and Monroe are going."

"How's it going with that guy?"

"Better than expected," I admitted. "So far, at least."

"What are you guys doing at the Racquet Club?"

"Observing. Watching. Maybe catch someone with their pants down. Maybe catch someone having a French dip sandwich and discussing Oprah's latest book club selection with their girlfriends."

Marina shrugged. "One or the other."

"Yep," I said. "Had to explain that to Monroe. He couldn't wait … and I quote him directly … to 'nail that bitch.'"

"Ouch."

"Yeah."

We drank our libations and were quiet for a few moments.

"I can't wait until all this is over," Marina said.

"Been tough?"

"It has. Trying to be strong for everyone else makes it infinitely harder to be strong for myself."

"Anybody helping out?"

"Well, you know, they try," Marina said. "But sometimes they try too hard and end up making things more difficult. And sometimes, they just want to be *seen* as trying and that makes it even worse. Fucking family politics. They're the worst."

"How many are there?"

"People? Last count was ninety-seven."

"Jesus."

"Yeah, it's a lot. At least, so far, we've avoided any drunken fights in hotel hallways but, you know, we still have another day to get through."

"Want me to send Puño down there?" I said. "Keep them all in line?"

Marina laughed and it did my heart good. "Yeah, could you?" she said. "Make my life a whole lot easier."

We sipped and stared into each other's pixelated eyes. After a moment, I tore myself away. "All right," I said. "I better get to bed. Big day tomorrow."

"Yeah, really rough," Marina said. "Lunching at the Lemon Grove Racquet Club. Have a lamb chop for me."

I gave her a soft laugh and said, "Love you, honey."

"Love you, too. Be careful, Brace."

"Roger that," I said. "Good night."

And the screen went blank.

CHAPTER THIRTEEN

As we had planned, Mongo dropped Monroe off at my office at ten o'clock sharp and the producer and I drove the twenty miles to the Lemon Grove Club together in the Camaro. I didn't think Club Security would allow the Camry past the front gate.

The Club was nestled between the Santa Paula Freeway and the usually bone-dry Santa Clara River. We turned left off the main road and drove down a nicely maintained drive that was bordered on either side by farmlands. I tried to ascertain what was growing there but couldn't be sure from the car. I guessed it was either strawberries or radishes.

The road ahead of us was lined with eucalyptus trees on each side, most of them towering to what seemed to be 100 feet or more. The tops of the trees leaned inward toward the road, creating the illusion of a tunnel leading to the Club. Finally, we came to a clearing, and it was if the whole world had opened wide.

We pulled into a ludicrously spacious parking lot, and I heard Monroe utter a whispered, "Wow," as the Clubhouse came into view. It looked like one of those glorious mansions you would find in the South, rising nobly, a gleaming white monument, surrounded with a perfectly manicured, perfectly green, lawn. A series of Roman columns supported a heavy wooden canopy that encircled the entire building, while the main door was marked with a soaring archway that cradled the door like a bird in a nest. Out of the gray-tiled roof there sprouted a white-painted dormer, probably the size of most people's apartments, its glass observation windows looking out over the lawn, the parking lot, and the racquet courts.

Behind the main building on the right was another structure, considerably less elaborate than the first building and apparently designed more for residential purposes. I assumed this is where the offices were, the storage rooms and perhaps a bedroom or two for those rare overnight guests.

To the left of the structure were the racquet courts, encircled by a tall chain link fence that was woven through with green fence slats to cut down wind and increase privacy. There were perhaps a dozen courts of various shapes and sizes. A sign demanding PICKLEBALL ON COURTS 4 AND 5 ONLY told me at least one of the sports intended. Tennis would be another, and maybe badminton, but that's where the limits of my racquet sports knowledge came to an end.

I pulled into the parking lot and took a spot that allowed us the best view of the entry road as well as the front entrance of the building. I killed the engine and sat back, adjusting the visor so that the sun didn't burn into my eyes.

"What do we do now?" Monroe said after a moment.

"Now, we wait," I said.

"We wait?"

"We wait," I said. "And we see what happens."

"Well, that doesn't sound very exciting," Monroe said. "That's because it isn't," I told him.

As we waited, I took inventory of the cars parked around us. There weren't many at this hour, maybe eight or nine in all. Of course, they were all ridiculously expensive vehicles. Most of them were SUVs built by companies that once were better known for their sportscars. I saw a Mercedes Benz GLS, a Porsche Cayenne and a Fiat 500X. There were a couple of huge pick-up trucks as well: A Ford F-450 and a Dodge Ram 1500 (the Longhorn Edition, whatever the hell that meant). The other vehicles more of the sportier type. There was a BMW Z4, a Toyota Supra and a Jaguar, the model of which I didn't recognize. All were late models (probably this year), and all were convertibles. All appeared to have been freshly washed and waxed … and I mean, like this morning.

Not a Chevy Camaro among them. The rich seemed to have no taste.

The only other car in the lot was a 2007 Toyota Pick-up but its presence was explained by the collection of yard tools in its bed. I glanced around to see if I could find the gardener at work, but he must have been behind the building or out by the courts out of sight.

"I assume we're waiting for Mrs. Wilder to show up," Monroe said.

"That's right."

"But how do we know she's even coming today?"

"We don't," I said. "We can assume that from the days she posts photos of food on her Facebook page, but we don't know for certain that's her routine. We're just guessing."

"Why do people do that?"

"Do what?"

"Post pictures of their food on their Facebook page? I mean, what do I care what they had for lunch?"

I shrugged. "I'm the last one you should be asking about social media," I said.

A car pulled into the parking lot from the road. Monroe sat up. "Is that her?"

I grinned. "Why don't we let them park first and we'll find out?"

"Yeah," Monroe said, deflating. "Sorry."

It was a red Cadillac CT5 sedan, although I'm sure the color had a fancier name— something like Sunset Crimson or Flaming Geranium. It, too, appeared to have been washed and waxed about half an hour ago. The driver was the only person in the car, but it was a woman and might even be our Mrs. Wilder.

It wasn't. The woman who climbed out of the Cadillac after parking it near one of those mammoth pickups was at least twenty years younger than Mrs. Wilder. She wore tight clothes that made it appear that she was going horseback riding. Her long, jet-black hair rippled down her back almost to her waist.

I glanced at the photo of Mrs. Wilder I'd stuck to the dash with a piece of Scotch tape. She stared back at me with the eyes of a woman who had experienced much more in her life than the thirty-year-old who just climbed out of that Cadillac. And Mrs. Wilder's hair was shoulder-length, brunette and touched with gray.

"That's not her," Monroe said.

"Nope."

We sat through a half dozen more arriving vehicles, all very expensive and all shiny clean, and an hour later we still had no Mrs. Wilder.

"Maybe she's not coming today," Monroe said.

"Maybe."

'What then?"

"We come back tomorrow."

Monroe sighed and let his shoulders droop. This wasn't the thrilling life of a private detective he'd seen in the movies.

But that was about to change.

Another Cadillac pulled into the parking lot, this one a hulking Escalade, pearly white (or Heaven's Cloud or Winter Justice or whatever the hell the marketers called it). It slipped into a slot near the Jaguar and the driver killed the engine.

Monroe was sitting up straight and staring at the driver's door. "I don't want to jinx it," he said. "But that might be our gal."

He was right. As the Escalade had pulled in, I had noted the similarities to the driver and the photo on my dashboard.

We watched as the Escalade door opened and a woman stepped out into the parking lot. She was about 5'2", probably 110 pounds and had brunette hair that fell just past her shoulders. I glanced at the photo in front of me again and nodded.

"Mrs. Wilder," I said to Monroe.

"That's her," he agreed.

Mrs. Wilder wore a pair of tan slacks that stopped just above her ankles with a wide black belt encircling her waist. Her shoes were a darker tan leather and appeared to be sensible with a small but obvious heel. Her light brown top looked like some sort of cashmere sweater, and the sleeves were ridiculously long, hanging over and hiding her hands. I guess that's a style. I wished Marina were here so she could tell me where Mrs. Wilder had purchased those clothes and who she was wearing.

"Looks like Louis Vuitton," Monroe said. "The pants, at least. Top might be Tom Ford. Shit ain't cheap, I can tell you that."

I gave him a look.

"Don't recognize the shoes," he said.

I smiled.

"Hey, what can I tell ya?" Monroe said. "I'm into fashion. Gotta be. Hollywood player and all."

He laughed and punched me in the arm. I let it go. This time.

Mrs. Wilder locked up her vehicle and headed through the front door of the Club. I took a few shots of her from my phone as she did. A moment later, she was inside, and it was just me and Monroe again.

"And now?" Monroe said.

"And now we wait," I said again.

"Seriously?" Monroe said. "Surely there's something else we can be doing."

"Well, we can't get into the Club," I said. "We're not members and these places are very strict about that. So, we have to sit here and wait till she comes back out. Hope she comes out with somebody. Maybe her new squeeze."

"Maybe not," Monroe said.

I laughed. "Now you're getting it," I said. "Maybe not."

"Then what?"

"Then we'll follow her to wherever she heads next," I told him. "See if she goes to the grocery store or some seedy hotel."

Monroe sat for a moment, apparently turning things over in his mind.

"Who says we can't get into the Club?" he asked and, before I could stop him, he had opened his door, climbed out of the Camaro, and was walking to the main door.

I rolled down my window and stuck my head out. "Monroe! Get back here!"

He held up a single finger. Mouthed the word "wait."

"Monroe!"

He stepped up to the main door, looked at me and gave a quick nod, and then was inside.

CHAPTER FOURTEEN

It had been over an hour since Monroe had entered the Lemon Grove Racquet Club. The good news is that the police hadn't shown up to haul away an intruder. The bad news is that I didn't know what the hell he was doing in there.

Many cars had come, and many cars had gone, but none of them had been Mrs. Wilder's. She was still inside, too.

I had taken a walk around the parking lot and the tennis courts but found nothing of interest. It was more to blow off steam than it was to investigate, I realized, because Shale Monroe was really pissing me off.

At two o'clock the main door opened, and Monroe came out. He shook hands with someone I couldn't see and then came my way. He locked eyes with mine and gave me a shit-eating grin.

A moment later, he was in the passenger seat beside me but before I could unleash the torrent of fury that had built up inside me, he turned to me and said, "Well, she's definitely having an affair."

I felt as though the wind had been knocked out of me.

"What?" I said weakly.

"Mrs. Wilder. She's definitely having an affair. I got some photos. She spent the entire time in there at a table with some dude. Wasn't her husband, I can tell you that much."

He waggled his phone at me.

"I got some photos. Wanna see?"

"Wait," I said. "Hold up. What the hell happened in there?"

Monroe smiled. "I went in. Asked to speak to the membership coordinator. Took forever for him to come

111

talk to me. Must be a bitch to get membership here. Anyway, I told him who I was and that I was considering becoming a member here. Stupid expensive, too. Six grand a year and three hundred a month. To play tennis?! Freaking crazy."

"Monroe," I said patiently. "Tell me about Mrs. Wilder."

"Yeah, yeah," he said. "So, once they find out I'm Shale Monroe the movie producer and that I might be interested in membership, the world became my oyster, you know? I got the grand tour, was introduced to a few of the guests and they even offered me free lunch. But I declined, you know. Wasn't gonna eat a free lunch with you sitting out here waiting."

I rolled my finger, telling him to go on.

"Anyway, while we're in the dining room, I see Mrs. Wilder sitting over in the corner, at a table with this dark, handsome, Don Ameche type." He gave me a look. "You know Don Ameche?"

I nodded. "I know Don Ameche," I said.

"Good," Monroe said. "Anyway, they were having a pretty heavy conversation, at least as far as I could tell. You know, I could hear their voices, but I couldn't make out the words. But they were moving their hands around and leaning together a lot to make their points. Like I said, I got a couple of photos. You wanna see them?"

He handed me his phone and I had to give it right back to him so he could enter his security code. "Sorry," he said, and handed it back.

I opened the photo app and swiped to the latest photos. They weren't very clear.

"Kinda blurry," I said.

"Yeah, I had to take them on the sly, you know? Didn't want to get caught taking pictures."

I nodded and looked closely at the photos. There were six in all and there was Mrs. Wilder, all right, sitting at a corner table with windows behind her, tall white drapes blocking off the view of the courts outside. I pinched the screen and zoomed in on the man. "Dark, handsome type" was the best description we were going to get. The photo was drenched in shadows and even brightening the image didn't help. The man's face simply went from a black glob to a white one.

"Were they holding hands?" I asked. "Was there any PDA?"

"No," Monroe said. "Not that I saw."

"So maybe he was just a friend," I said. "Maybe even a business associate."

"Maybe," Monroe agreed. "But it sure didn't feel that way. I mean, they were off in that little corner together, the only place where it was kinda dark inside, and they had the drapes closed even though it was a really glorious day out there. Why wouldn't you want to see it?"

I nodded. "But you couldn't hear what they were saying."

Monroe shook his head. "No. Just their voices. Couldn't understand the words."

I gave him his phone back. "Well, that doesn't give us much," I said. "But it's more than we started with."

Forty minutes later, Mrs. Wilder came out of the building, alone, walked to her car, started it up and drove away.

After a few minutes, we took up the chase.

CHAPTER FIFTEEN

It was a boring chase. We followed Mrs. Wilder and her Escalade and found out she liked to buy wine at Grocery Outlet, her favorite department at the Goodwill Thrift Store was Women's Fashions and that she drove the speed limit and not a mile over everywhere she went.

The clock on the dashboard told me it was nearly four o'clock. We were parked on the street in front of a florist. Mrs. Wilder was inside, presumedly buying flowers.

"She'll be heading home next," I told Monroe. "We might as well call it a day."

"Sounds good to me," Monroe said. "Don't take this the wrong way, but I'm kind of sick sitting in this car all day."

"That makes two of us."

I punched the ENGINE START STOP button and the Camaro roared to life. "Where are you and Mongo having dinner tonight?"

"I told him I feel like Mexican food," Monroe said. "He found this place called Casa de Soria."

"Had that just the other night," I said. "You'll enjoy it. Make sure and get a margarita."

I dropped him off near the front entrance of the Pierpont Inn just as dusk was settling. The sun was putting on the world's greatest light show as it sank into the Pacific Ocean.

"Listen, I assume you don't work weekends," Monroe said.

"You assume wrong," I told him. "There's no 9-to-5 in the private detective business."

"Oh," Monroe said. "They're expecting me on set through Monday." He shrugged. "But I can cancel. Have someone fill in for me."

"No, don't' do that," I told him. "This is one of those rare weekends that I didn't plan on working."

"Why don't you come down?" Monroe asked. "Check it out. Shadow *me* this time."

"Thanks," I said. "But I don't think so."

"Come on, it'll be fun." He wiggled his eyebrows. "I'll introduce you to Rosario Dawson. She's our lead."

"It's tempting, but I got stuff to do," I told him. "And remember, I'm off Tuesday and Wednesday for the funeral but I'll be back to the office on Thursday, the usual time."

"Got it," Monroe said. "Good luck down there."

I nodded. "Think I'm gonna need it."

I took my foot off the brake and the Camaro lunged forward and I heard Monroe yell out, "Hey!"

I stopped the car. Monroe came over and stuck his head in the window. "Listen," he said. "I'm having a little soiree at my Calabasas home next Friday. Why don't you and the Mrs. come on down?" I started to protest but he cut me off. "I know it's been a tough week for the two of you and it's only gonna get tougher. A little party with the stars might take some of the edge off. Might be just what you need."

"I'll think about it," I said. "See what Marina says."

"Yeah, do that," Monroe said, stepping away. "It'll be fun, I promise."

I headed home.

CHAPTER SIXTEEN

It was just me and Wurzel for the weekend which meant a lot of fast food for me and a lot of begging for fast food for Wurzel.

I did have one appointment I had to keep. Andy Larsen, my old pal from the Ventura County Post newspaper, had invited me to lunch and we'd agreed to meet at Winchester's, just a few doors up from my building.

Andy was sitting at the bar waiting for me when I walked in at just before eleven. There was no missing him. His 350-pound girth overflowed the unfortunate barstool he was perched on, and his bald spot gleamed like a silver beacon in the overhead lights. There was a scattering of food items and crumpled cloth napkins in front of him in an arrangement that could only be called a mess. A half-empty beer glass rose from the center of that mess, and I knew that, despite the fact it probably wasn't his first, it most certainly would not be his last.

"What's up, numb-nuts," I said, taking the seat next to him.

"'bout time," Andy said. "I've been here twenty minutes."

I glanced at my watch. "I thought we said eleven," I told him.

"We did," Andy said. "Just fucking with you."

The bartender, whose name tag announced she was Barbara, came over and I ordered a Chief Peak from Topa Topa Brewing. Andy made a face.

"How can you drink that bitter shit?"

"How can you drink that pissy yellow beer?" I said, pointing at the glass in front of him. "What is that? Miller Lite?"

"Lucky guess," Andy said, unimpressed.

Barbara returned with my Chief Peak, and I took an appreciative sip. Andy wasn't wrong. It was a bitter beer, but I'll take a beer with flavor over a beer that tastes like weak tea any day.

"Let's order," Andy said. "I'm starving."

I glanced at the two empty plates and their errant crumbs on the bar in front of him but didn't say anything. Andy ordered the Belt Burger and I opted for the Black Butte Porter Tri-tip chili. Barbara wrote down our orders and wandered away.

"You give me shit about my beer choices," I said. "And then you order a hamburger with a fried egg on it?"

"It's good."

"Yeah, I don't think so."

I drank some beer and Andy finished his, wiggling his empty glass when Barbara passed for another.

"So, what's new in the Dick business?" Andy asked.

"Not much," I told him. "Same ol', same ol'."

"Whatever happened to that guy who was ripping off the insurance company?" Andy asked. "You know. That personal trainer?"

I sipped some beer and smiled. Because the beer was good and so was Andy's question.

"Oh, that guy," I said. "I followed that jerk around for a whole week and every single day he did something that no one with a fractured disc would have been able to do. He didn't even really try to hide it. I got photos of him working out at the gym and trimming the trees in his yard. On a ladder. He even helped his friends move a refrigerator. Upstairs."

"Refrigerators are the worst," Andy said. "Always pay someone to do that for you."

"My thoughts exactly. Anyway, I turned in all that stuff to the insurance company and they went after him. And the son of a bitch tried to convince them it wasn't him!"

Andy looked at me with disbelief. "Even with all those photos?"

"Even with all those photos."

"So, what happened to him?"

"That's the part that sucks," I said. "I don't know. Usually, they don't tell me. Sometimes, they'll call on me to testify or something, but most of the time I'm out of the loop."

Andy nodded. "That does suck."

"What's up in the newspaper world?" I asked.

Andy shook his head. "Fuckin' paper gets smaller every day. In the old days, you private dicks could sit in the lobby and hold an open newspaper in front of you, and it'd cover your whole face. Nobody would know who was behind it. These days, you hold up the open newspaper, and it's like holding a fucking pamphlet in front of you. Doesn't hide anything. Everybody can see right past it. I guess the good news is that there's no need to cut out eyeholes, like they did in the old days."

"Yeah," I said. "I'm pretty sure nobody ever really did that."

"I saw it somewhere," Andy said. "Must've happened."

"What about online?"

"Online's a bitch," Andy said. "Harder to get advertising dollars. Everyone wants to see your numbers, you know? Your web traffic, your number of individual users. Your click-throughs." He laughed. "And if you think it's hard to hide behind an open newspaper, try hiding behind an iPad!"

Barbara brought our food and we dug in. The pungent stench of fried egg on Andy's burger almost took my appetite away. I just don't get fried eggs. My chili, however, was outstanding and the egg stink was soon forgotten.

"What are you working on now?" Andy asked between massive bites of burger.

"Cheating spouse case," I said, wiping chili from my chin. "Maybe."

"Maybe?"

"Yeah, just maybe," I said. "I'd say that seventy percent of the people who come to me thinking their spouse is cheating on them are wrong. People are just tired, man. They work all day, they come home, they clean the house, they make dinner, they fix the car, whatever. They're tired at the end of the evening. Too often, people think that just because they're not getting laid three times a week, that their spouse is cheating."

"You ever get a gay man coming in, saying his husband is cheating?" Andy asked.

"Why?" I asked him. "You dating a married man?"

"Hell, no," Andy said. "I've got enough baggage in my life. Don't need someone else's. Or their husband's."

I ate another spoonful of chili. It had a hefty chunk of tri-trip on it. It was delightful.

"Once or twice," I said. "There was this guy from Camarillo came in once, told me he knew his husband was cheating. I asked him how he knew, and he told me that he smelled *woman* on him."

Andy shot me a look.

"That's a direct quote," I continued. "'I smell *woman* on him.'"

"And was he?"

"Cheating?"

"Yeah."

"He was," I said. "With a woman. Broke his husband's heart."

"Sad," Andy said.

"Yeah," I agreed.

We ordered another beer when Barbara came by again and Andy ordered something aptly called Chocolate Death

Cake. I worried about the man's health as he wolfed it down.

We finished our beers and chatted about our lives for a moment. He was appropriately condolent when I told him that Marina's mother had passed.

"There is one other thing," I said. "But you can't print this, okay?"

Andy looked intrigued. "Okay."

"Shale Monroe is here, shadowing me," I said.

"Shale Monroe? The movie producer?" Andy had started his career in journalism as a film reviewer and was a life-long movie fan, a trait we shared. I knew he'd know Shale Monroe's name.

"That's the guy," I said. "Doing research for a possible … are you ready for this? … Shorts and Sandals Detective movie."

Andy gave me a disbelieving eye. "You're shitting me."

I shook my head, sharing his disbelief. "I am not," I said.

"Fucking L.A. Times," Andy said. "I shoulda wrote that story. Got a movie deal. Not some dweeb who doesn't even know you. *I'm* your best friend, goddammit."

"Well …"

"How long's he here for?" Andy asked.

"Another week or two. I can ask him if he'd be interested in talking with you once we're done."

"Yeah, why not," Andy said. "Although he probably can't. Probably got some L.A. Times exclusive agreement or something." He took another sip of his dwindling beer. "What's he like, this guy? Is he anything like his showbiz persona?"

I thought back to the interviews I'd seen before I met Shale Monroe, to the news stories of his all-day parties, his flings with A-List actresses and supermodels, and his rousing adventures when filming in strange parts of the world where no one had been for hundreds of years.

And I thought of Shale Monroe in my office, eager to get out and see what a detective does. Especially one in shorts and sandals.

"Pretty much the same," I said. "A little lower key, I guess, but then he's here in Ventura with me, not in the bowels of the Amazon Rain Forest with George Clooney and Jessica Chastain."

"Yeah, see if you can set up an interview," Andy said. "What the hell."

"I'll ask," I told him.

Andy finished his beer, wiped his hands on a cloth napkin. "You got this, Dick?" he said.

"What? You invited me."

"Yeah, but I think you owe me," Andy said.

I probably did.

"Yeah, I got it," I said.

"Gotta go," Andy said, standing. "Interviewing a new photographer this afternoon. That's the thing about the online edition. Everyone wants to see a photo. I'm not even sure anyone reads the goddamn prose anymore, but they love the freaking pictures."

"It's a new world," I said.

"Yeah," Andy agreed. "But I'm not sure it's a better one."

CHAPTER SEVENTEEN

I enjoyed a leisurely Sunday with Wurzel, a couple more of those bitter beers, a BBQ Bacon Cheeseburger Pizza from Pizza Hut (that Marina would *never* know about) and a few more episodes of *Voyage to the Bottom of the Sea*. Wurzel desperately wanted a slice of pizza to call his own, but I had to limit him to a small chunk of BBQ'd bacon. At one point, I called Marina just to check in, but she didn't pick up. I left a message for her telling her I loved her and asking her to give me a call if she needed me. She wouldn't call. Marina had it all under control. She usually did.

Next thing I knew, it was Monday again and I found myself back in the office, willing the phone to ring, and thinking about Puño's ex, Cassandra, and a guy named Locke.

The fact is that I knew quite a bit about Cassandra but knew nothing about Locke, the least of which is where did he get a name like Locke? With Monroe still "on set" the day was all mine, so I decided to make use of the free time to educate myself regarding Mr. Locke Reynolds.

As usual, I started with the Private Detective's Best Friend. According to Google, Locke Reynolds of Ventura had a Facebook account (everyone did, whether they admitted it or not), a Twitter feed, a LinkedIn profile, and an Instagram blog. His Facebook account was loaded with pictures of Locke at the beach, usually standing beside a surfboard, never standing on one. There were also a few shots of him and Cassandra out and about, mostly at local restaurants, and one video of an English Bulldog catching a wave on a boogie board.

According to his Twitter account, his last tweet had been over two years ago and was an uninspired diss about the Dallas Cowboys: *Are you scared of catching the flu? Just hang in the Cowboys' end zone, they don't catch anything there.*

His LinkedIn profile, however, told me that he was a construction worker and heavy equipment operator and that he was General Foreman for the Pheonix Construction company in Fillmore. I assumed they misspelled "Phoenix" for marketing purposes. Kind of like Def Leppard, Motley Crue, Snoop Dogg or Ludacris.

Locke also hinted that he was available for side jobs but didn't come right out and say it. I figured that might violate his employee agreement with Pheonix Construction Company.

Google also told me that Locke was a clinical psychologist based out of Chicago, Illinois and that he was a partner with an equity firm that specialized in food space investments. Apparently, there was more than one Locke Reynolds walking the planet.

I entered "Pheonix Construction" and "Fillmore, CA" in the search box and got a message stating *Showing results for 'phoenix construction' 'fillmore, ca' Search instead for 'pheonix construction' 'fillmore, ca'*. Irritated both at Google's sterile efficiency and at Pheonix Construction company for their ridiculous misspelling, I chose the latter search.

An address on Goodenough Road in Fillmore popped up and I printed it out on the ancient laser printer in the corner. The name of the road gave me a little smile. I don't know if Pheonix Construction Company was looking for a new motto, but I came up with one after just a quick glance at the street name: PHEONIX CONSTRUCTION COMPANY: NOT GREAT, BUT GOODENOUGH.

I decided if they liked it, they could have it for free.

Thirty-five minutes later, I pulled the Camry up to what was basically an open lot, encircled by a chain link fence and an aluminum sign identifying the location as PHEONIX CONSTRUCTION COMPANY. There was a cartoon drawing of the legendary bird on the sign as well, with its murderously misspelled name painted in cursive writing just below his beak: *Pheobe*. It took a Herculean effort not to pull out a permanent marker and cross that shit out.

Construction equipment of all sizes and shapes littered the property and surrounded a two-doored mobile trailer in the center that I deftly identified as the office. The giant

sign with the word OFFICE painted on it in two-foot letters was also a clue. There were cement mixers, wheel load-
ers and bulldozers scattered everywhere, all parked at crazy
angles as though they'd been tossed there by a child. A trio
of white Toyota pick-ups emblazoned with dyslexic
PHEONIX CONSTRUCTION banners on their doors
sat unattended near the office.

I climbed out of the Camry and stood a moment, enjoying the warm morning sun on my face. I walked past
another, smaller sign that happily stated OF COURSE,
WE'RE OPEN, and went through the chain link gate.
Gravel crunched beneath my feet as I passed a John Deere
wheel loader, a Marshalltown mixer, and the Toyota pick-
ups.

The metal steps leading up to the office creaked and
swayed beneath my weight. They weren't so much attached
to the trailer as just sitting beside it. It felt like the whole
unit might slide out from underneath me at any moment.

I pulled open the thin aluminum door and stepped in.
Inside, it was something like you'd see in the movies. There
were towers of paper stacked on every available surface.

Most of it looked like reports, the kind run by managers with nothing better to do than print reports. There were a couple of chairs strewn about seemingly at random and on one end was a large metal desk, overflowing with reports that were stacked high and leaning like a particular tower in Italy. There was a woman behind the desk with what first looked like a cigarette poking out of the corner of her mouth. She was in her fifties, I'd guess late fifties, and she wore a flowery top that was so faded I thought maybe she was wearing it inside out.

It seemed she was here alone.

"Help you?" the woman said, expelling a cloud of vapor that almost instantly filled the entire room. It wasn't a cigarette, I realized, but a vaping device. The sickly-sweet odor of overripe strawberries suddenly filled the air.

"I hope so," I said, walking over and extending my hand. "Archie Leach, OSHA."

She didn't seem impressed with the "Archie Leach," but the "OSHA" got her attention. Her eyes widened slightly, and she slowly lowered the vaping device beneath her desk.

"I'm following up on a complaint," I continued. "Mind if I sit?" I did so without waiting for an answer.

"What kind of complaint?"

"That is, of course, confidential," I said. "Miss …?"

"Berger. Mrs. Carol Berger."

"Pleased to meet you, Mrs. Berger," I said. "I'm sure you understand. Confidentiality is very important in cases like this."

"Of course."

"But I'm sure you're willing to cooperate in every way, right? I mean, you wouldn't want to get in the way of a government investigation, would you?"

Her eyes widened even more, and she shot me a glance. "I think I should talk to Mr. Reynolds," she said, and reached for the black, old-fashioned telephone on her desk.

"Would that be Mr. Locke Reynolds?"

She paused. "Um. Yes."

"The General Foreman?"

She nodded.

"Then let's *not* call *him*," I said, gently pushing down the receiver. "If you know what I mean."

It took her a second, but then Mrs. Berger nodded. "Oh," she said, and nodded her head slowly.

"Tell me about him," I prodded. "Is he a good boss? I mean, I assume he's your boss."

Mrs. Berger nodded. "Well, yes," she said. "He and Mr. Davis. Mr. Davis is the owner."

"I see. And how long have you worked with Mr. Reynolds?"

Mrs. Berger's eyes looked up into her head. "I guess about six years now," she said, counting silently. "Yes, six years."

"And how's he been? Is he a good boss? A nice man?"

"Oh, yes," Mrs. Berger said. "Very much so. He and Mr. Davis have been very good to me."

"Have you ever seen him get angry?" I asked. "Snap at somebody? Maybe throw something?"

Mrs. Berger's eyebrows came down. "Throw something ...?" she said quietly. "I'm sorry, sir, what did you say your name was again?"

"Leach, Archie Leach," I told her. "OSHA."

"Do you have … ID?"

"We'll get to that later," I told her. "First, you were saying you saw him throw something."

"No, you said that."

"What did he throw?"

"He didn't throw anything."

"But he's got a temper?"

"No, I didn't say that, either!" Mrs. Berger said. "He's a nice guy. Very seldom yells."

"But he does yell?"

"Well, of course," Mrs. Berger continued. "What man doesn't? They all lose their temper sometimes. Things go wrong. People screw up."

"You've seen him yell at someone?" I asked.

"Well, yes," she said. "But never someone who didn't deserve it." She thought for a moment. "There was that time when he had Armando in here, one of our drivers. Armando got too close to some scaffolding on a job. Scraped up the side of the truck and bent the scaffolding all to hell, too." She shook her head. "Mr. Reynolds read him the riot act, right here in this office," she said. "Raised holy hell with him, told him he might be fired. It was a safety issue. And because of the insurance, you know, and the truck repairs."

"Sure, sure," I said. "And what happened to Armando?"

"He straightened up," she said. "Mr. Reynolds hasn't had to yell at him again since."

"But he didn't throw anything at him?"

"No!' Mrs. Berger said. "Why do you keep bringing that up?"

"No reason," I said. "Where is Mr. Reynolds now?"

"He's out on a job," Mrs. Berger told me.

"I assumed that," I said. "I want to know where."

"I'm not sure I should tell you," Mrs. Berger said slowly.

"Is that so?" I said. "Are you afraid I'll catch him throwing something?"

"No!" she said again. "But it just doesn't seem right that you're … I don't know … sneaking up on him. Spying on him."

"Mrs. Berger," I said. "OSHA does not sneak. We do not spy. This is a government investigation. I need to see Mr. Reynolds in action. I need to observe him in the workplace." I gave her a sorrowful look. "Please don't make me take this to the next level. I don't want to go to my boss and tell him you weren't cooperative. And you don't want me to do that, either."

She stared at me silently for a moment and I could see the wheels of her mind working. Finally, after a full thirty seconds, she grabbed a yellow Post-It note cube from her desk, peeled off a page, and wrote down an address.

"He's at this job site," she said. "It's a commercial site. They're building a Starbucks, or something."

"Of course, they are," I said, taking the Post-It note from her. "When are they not?"

I stood. "All right. I'm on my way. I thank you, Mrs. Berger, and the State of California thanks you as well.

I walked to the door and turned back. Her hand was already on the phone receiver. "Do not call him," I told her. "Do not tell him I'm coming."

I stepped out of the trailer onto the rickety stairway, closed the door behind me and walked down to the ground level. A pang of guilt ran through me. I had played Mrs. Berger like the proverbial fiddle, and she was probably a very nice woman, completely innocent of any wrongdoing. But I knew she was already on the phone with Locke Reynolds, and I hadn't even made it to the street yet. I kept my fingers crossed that he wasn't a Cary Grant fan and recognized the legendary actor's real name.

Not that it mattered. I was on my way to the job site—it was in Santa Paula just a few miles away—but I had no intention of speaking with him. I was just going to watch from the street, see what I could see. Of course, he'd be on his best behavior now that he was expecting me, or rather an OSHA inspector, so I wouldn't be seeing the *real* Locke Reynolds, not at first. Eventually, however, he'll assume that OSHA wasn't showing up after all and slip back into his usual ways. Hopefully, then, I'd catch him off guard, see what he was really like on the job, and maybe I'd learn something interesting about him.

Maybe he'd even throw something at somebody.

CHAPTER EIGHTEEN

I stopped at a BBQ place on Harvard Boulevard and ordered a hot link sandwich and a bowl of BBQ beans. Then I drove over to the job site and parked across the street near a thrift store.

The job site was on the corner of Harvard and another street whose sign has mysteriously been sheared off the pole. I ventured a guess that a big rig had taken the corner too closely and peeled the sign off the pole like it was paper. Maybe it had even been Armando. But it could have just been stolen, too. Sometimes, people take weird souvenirs.

Like the Pheonix yard itself, the job site was surrounded by a wobbly chain link fence and packed with construction equipment and supplies. The wooden frame of a
single-story building rose from its center, rising only near
the front where I assumed the name of the business would
soon be emblazoned. From what I could make out, there
was a storefront with an awning on the side, beneath which
a drive-through could be constructed. I couldn't tell if they
were building a Starbucks, a Chick-Fil-A or a drive-through
dentist office (which seemed unlikely) but the site was
busy, with men buzzing around carrying plywood, 2x4s,
and hand tools at a steady pace. The pop-pop-pop of elec-
tric hammers filled the air.

At first glance, it seemed that all the workers on site
wore the same type of clothes, boots, and hard hats. I was
concerned that it was going to be difficult locating Locke
amongst them in a weird *Where's Waldo?* kind of way. It
wound up being far easier than I expected when a man
wearing blue-jeans, a safety-orange t-shirt, and a white hard
hat—virtually identical to what everyone else on site was
wearing—came bounding out of the single-door office and

hopped down the aluminum stairs. A large graphic sticker on the side of his hard hat clearly identified him as Locke Reynolds.

It was the stylized skull of The Punisher logo.

I watched him step down onto the dirt and come to a halt. He scanned the perimeter, checking for any new faces, particularly one of Archie Leach, OSHA inspector. After a moment, apparently satisfied that there were no arrivals, Leach headed toward the wooden structure frame.

It was impossible to hear anything that was being said on site due to my location and the hum of traffic and the chatter of power tools, so I sat in the front seat of the Camry and ate my hot link sandwich and beans. The sandwich was amazing, the sausage spicy and the accompanying hot sauce hotter than expected but still delicious. The beans were perhaps better, reminding me of campsites and fire-cooked dinners consumed by kerosene light. Initially, I had considered the name of the place, BEST BBQ, to be an indication of a businessman's lack of creativity. Now I realized there was no better name.

It took about two hours before Locke stopped looking over his shoulder and expecting OSHA to arrive. He seemed to relax, his movements becoming more fluid, his interactions with others taking on a new vibrancy. He was like a reality TV star who suddenly forgot the cameras hovering around him and became himself. That was always a good thing for the audience. Not always for the person in front of the camera.

I watched Locke as he dealt with questions from the on-site foreman, as he directed a group of workers to go around back and get to work on the other side of the building frame. I watched as he disappeared into the small trailer once or twice to deal with a phone call or other issue. There must have been no bathroom in the tiny trailer office because Locke used the puke green outhouse with the ANOTHER ANDY GUMP; THERE IS A DIFFERENCE sign on the door, at least two, maybe three times. Once, Locke had to wait almost three minutes before the worker before him finished. They exchanged words and then laughed as they passed one another.

I glanced at my watch. It was almost 4:30 PM. The workday was nearly over. I was certain that I was seeing the real Locke Reynolds now—not the Locke Reynolds who thought OSHA was watching him—and I'd really learned nothing. There had been no outbursts, no heated exchanges, and he hadn't thrown anything at anybody. What had I learned? That Locke didn't seem to be a hot-head, at least on the job.

I was seconds away from declaring the day a complete bust when one of those white Toyota pick-ups pulled up to the job site and stopped outside of the gate. As it waited, a worker from inside came over, unlatched the gate, and began to roll it open. Almost immediately, the truck lurched forward, its front end catching the side of the gate, and the worker inside leapt away as the gate jumped out of its guide and twisted away with a screech of stressed metal. The truck driver hit the brakes, hard, and the Toyota's tires gave a tiny screech as it came to a complete stop.

"Fuck!" I heard that from my place all the way over in the thrift store parking lot. The driver, who knew he was in a world of trouble.

Locke came jogging over as the driver climbed out of the truck to survey the damage. I sat up, thinking about what Mrs. Berger had told me when Armando had driven his truck into some scaffolding.

Mr. Reynolds read him the riot act, right here in this office. Raised holy hell with him, told him he might be fired.

This may have been what I'd been waiting for.

I hoped it wasn't poor Armando again.

Locke went first to the worker who had opened the gate. He touched his shoulder, appeared to be asking if he was all right. I saw the worker nod vigorously. No damage done.

Locke walked past the truck driver, not even acknowledging that he was there. He examined the damage to the gate and then the damage to truck. From where I sat, I could really see neither. It could have been mild, the gate simply off-track and the truck merely scratched, and it could have been worse. Perhaps the gate would have to be replaced rather than repaired, and the truck might have to have the front panel replaced. These days, even a small impact like this one could run you a few grand at the body shop.

Finally, after examining the damage from every angle and closely checking the truck tires, Locke seemed to indicate to the workers standing around looking to get back to work and get the gate back in place.

And then he turned swiftly, grabbed a hunk of the truck driver's shirt in his hands, and pulled him away from the vehicle. The driver's eyes went wide with fear.

I leaned forward even more, cocking my head, and getting as close to the open window as I could. If possible, I wanted to hear this.

I couldn't hear a thing. The traffic had only increased since I had first arrived, and now it was almost five o'clock. Rush hour.

I watched as Locke roughly dragged the truck driver over to the chain-link fence and shoved him against it. He forced the man into the fence so firmly that the metal netting bowed out into the street in a half-sphere like a stripper's thigh in a fishnet.

I could see Locke's face over the truck driver's shoulder, and it was a mask of anger and frustration. His mouth was working furiously and, even though I couldn't see it from where I sat, I knew spittle was flying. He poked a finger into the driver's chest and then pointed it directly at his face, leaning in, saying something with a nearly demonic sneer. Finally, he gave the worker a shove, pushing him deeper into the chain-link, and then let go of him, turned his back, and walked away.

I watched with sympathy as the truck driver slid down into a crouch, his hands on his knees. I could see him taking deep breaths and I knew he was trying to compose himself.

I know how he felt. I've been in that position myself. And it feels pretty shitty.

Locke went back to the gate and watched the workers there as they attempted to slip it back onto its guide. It seemed to slide back in easily and Locke nodded, satisfied. He turned and headed back to the tiny office, went up the rickety stairs, and disappeared inside.

I sat there for a while, quietly considering what I had just witnessed. What had I learned? Locke had a temper, a temper that sometimes manifested itself on the job. But so did I. So did Marina. So did Puño (well, of course, Puño).

But did that mean he was a wife-beater? A domestic abuser? Or did it mean he was just a crappy boss? It gave me something to think about over the next few days when I was in Los Angeles with Marina, in those sure to be many moments when she didn't need me.

I started the Camry and pulled away just as it appeared that the workers there had completed work on the gate. They were rolling it back and forth, open and closed, over and over, to make sure it was functioning properly, and they seemed to be congratulating one another on a job well done.

CHAPTER NINETEEN

The Cathedral of Our Lady of the Angels is one of the most magnificent buildings in Los Angeles, both inside and out. It was designed by Spanish architect Professor José Rafael Moneo and his vision of a vibrant, modern cathedral soars to eleven stories of majestic glory while its brave design features virtually no right angles, adding a sense of liquid spirituality and intrigue.

Esmeralda's funeral was traditionally solemn, untraditionally (and mercifully) short, and full of Catholic rituals and customs that I have never understood. When the mass was over, Marina's mother was interred beside her husband in the church's mausoleum, which was located one story beneath the cathedral.

As Marina stood beside me, stoically accepting the condolences of a seemingly never-ending line of family members, I bathed in the beauty surrounding us. The Southern Californian sun beamed through the glorious stained-glass windows surrounding us, lighting up the rich stone and marble walls and sarcophagi with a decidedly holy glow. It was enough to make one believe in God.

Marina's mother had insisted on a "happy event" upon her passing so Marina had booked a banquet hall just over a mile away for the wake. I think Esmeralda would have been pleased with the results. Friends and family gathered together and told funny and warm stories, laughing and crying at them all, while enjoying a buffet of Esmeralda's favorite foods, including chicken and carne asada street tacos, enchilada rojas and a pile of crunchy churros stacked like a Jenga game.

I did my best to be supportive and never left Marina's side as she gracefully accepted condolences, sympathy, and loving memories. She turned down my offers to retrieve food for her but accepted my invitation for wine. I knew that's what she needed most today: a little liquid fortification.

It was almost ten o'clock that evening before the last guests drifted away, a family of five from Durango who were Esmeralda's second cousins removed. In speedy Spanish, they offered Marina their warmest thoughts as I stood beside her and tried to look like I understood every word. I understood maybe every third word. A few minutes later, they were gone, and a cleaning crew suddenly materialized and began picking up our mess.

Marina stood silently, staring blankly at the door her relatives had just exited through. I moved closer, put my arm around her shoulders and said, "You okay?"

Her face crumpled into a sob so fast it scared me. She pressed her head against my chest and said, "No."

There was nothing I could do but hold her as the sobs harshly racked her body and five days of tension and grief bled out.

CHAPTER TWENTY

Marina came out of the shower, wearing the cotton robe provided by the hotel, just as the room service guy was leaving. She hadn't wanted to eat, claimed she wasn't hungry, but I told her that she needed to. I knew she hadn't eaten well since the day her mom had passed last week.

We pulled a couple of chairs over to the serving cart and I removed the silver domes from the plates. Marina was hungrier than she thought. She attacked the haystack of French fries as if she'd never eaten anything so delicious and then dug into her Cranberry Walnut Kale salad almost as though she was afraid somebody was going to take it away before she got her fill.

"You know," I told her. "If you want my hamburger, you can have that, too."

She smiled a little and it made my heart glad.

"Don't make offers you don't intend to keep," she said.

We ate mostly in silence, and she did, in fact, have a little of my hamburger. When we were done, I pushed the cart into the hallway outside as she switched on the TV and turned down the bed. Moments later, we were both beneath the covers watching Jimmy Kimmel talking with Gwyneth Paltrow about her toenails.

"You know what I regret?" Marina said.

"No. What's that?"

"I can't remember the last time I told my mother that I loved her."

"She knew …"

"I know she knew," Marina cut me off. "But I haven't said that to her in months." She bit her lip. "Maybe years."

I started to say "She knew" again but stopped myself. It seemed that Marina wanted to work this out herself.

"I talked to her every week," she said. "Every day, most weeks. And I never thought to tell her that. Never thought to just say, 'Mom, I love you.'"

"You were busy. She knew that. The words aren't what matters, it's the emotion." That's what I wanted to say, but I kept my mouth shut.

"I wish there was a way I could let her know," Marina said softly, and I realized she was drifting off to sleep. "I wish I could talk to her just one more time."

Her head tilted into the pillow and a split second later, she was out. A sleep she had earned more than anyone I had ever known.

I grabbed the remote (thinking about the article I'd read that said the TV remote is the filthiest thing in any hotel room), powered down the TV and then reached over and clicked off the lamp. I read e-mails on my phone for a few minutes and then put that down and rolled over.

It was only a few moments before I, too, was asleep.

CHAPTER TWENTY-ONE

The next morning, we slept in just a little bit and then got up to take on the day. Marina told me that we'd spend most of it saying goodbye to family. What she didn't tell me was that "saying goodbye to the family" meant helping them with their luggage, printing out their airline tickets and suggesting a good place to have breakfast.

Thankfully, not everyone stayed at the same hotel as Marina and I, so, instead of getting 97 people out and on their way, we only had to deal with about 40. By one o'clock, they were all heading back home, except for the folks from Durango who had decided that this was as good a time as any to visit Sea World. Using the hotel's business center, Marina helped them buy their tickets online and printed out a map so they could drive straight there. She even helped them pick out a hotel in the Gaslamp district that wasn't *too* expensive so they could enjoy their evening the day before they went to see Shamu and his friends.

Exhausted yet again, we decided to have a late lunch at the bar. I ordered a sourdough bacon sandwich and a Makers Mark neat and Marina asked for a plate of capellini and a glass of Sauvignon Blanc.

Our drinks came first, and we clinked glasses and took sips. "Tell me more about this Shale Monroe," Marina said.

"Not much to tell," I said. "He's eager and anxious but at least he seems to listen when I tell him to chill out." I gave a little laugh. "Well, most of the time."

"What does that mean?" Marina wanted to know.

I told her about the Lemon Grove Racquet Club and how Monroe's impatience turned into his impromptu interest in becoming a member. Marina laughed the heartiest I'd seen her in days.

"The worse thing is that it worked," I told her. "If he had been a better photographer, we might be done with that case by now."

Marina shook her head, amused. "And what about Puño?" she asked. "And Cassandra?"

"Only spent a little time on that one," I said. "Seen nothing so far."

Marina nodded. Our food came and we both ate silently. I ordered another Makers Mark and Marina asked for another wine. She'd drained the first one more quickly than usual, I noticed, but then she'd had one blue hell of a week.

She was halfway through her pasta when she said, "Brace, I'd like to ask you something." She didn't look up from her food, she didn't turn toward me. She just waited quietly until I replied.

"Sure," I said. "Of course. You know that."

"But I don't want you to judge me," she said.

Something twisted in my gut.

"Okay," I said.

"You know that psychic that works with the police department? The one that Steve works with?"

I knew who she was referring to. Millicent "Millie" Hawthorne. My old friend Lieutenant Steven Powell of the

Ventura Police Department had introduced me to her a few years back when he was working on the case of a missing boy. According to Powell, Millie had used her psychic ability to lead them directly to the boy, who had been buried alive on a lonely stretch of beach by his estranged father who wanted revenge on his soon-to-be-divorced wife. The boy was still alive when the VPD dug him out of the sand, and Steve swore to me that the outcome would have been much different if it hadn't been for Millie's lead.

I wasn't sure I believed in psychics. The conundrum was that I believed Steve Powell.

"Yeah," I said to Marina. I popped the last bit of bacon into my mouth and chewed. "I know her."

"I want to talk to her," Marina said. "Can you get me a meeting?"

That twist in my gut tightened but it was too soon to ask questions. "Sure," I told her. "I'll set something up."

"Thank you," Marina whispered. She put her fork into pasta, twirled it, and then let it drop into her plate. "You think I'm crazy, don't you?" she said suddenly.

"Why would I think that?" I asked. But I knew.

"Because I want to talk to that psychic," Marina said. "To see if she can contact mom."

I took a breath. "I don't think you're crazy," I said. "I think you're overwhelmed with grief and grief does weird things to us."

"What do you know about grief?" Marina said sharply. "Your parents are still alive."

I shot her a look. She held my eyes for a moment and then looked away, putting her face in her hands. A soft sob eased out of her. "I don't know, I don't know, I don't know," she droned between her fingers. "I don't know what to do."

The bartender came by, gave Marina a concerned glance, and removed our dishes. He gave me a look that asked, "Want another drink?" and I waved my hand at him. Not now. I waited until he had walked away. "Grief is like any other pain," I said at last. "No one but you can tell you how much it hurts." Marina moaned but kept her palms pressed to her eyes. "If it will help you deal with that grief, then I have no problem with you going to see Millicent," I continued. "But you need to manage your expectations. She doesn't talk to the dead."

Another soft moan and Marina took a deep, ragged breath. "I'm sorry," she said. "I'm sorry I said that about your parents."

"What? That they're not dead? How dare you!" I teased.

She took her hands away from her eyes and punched me gently in the arm, a weak, teary smile on her face. "You know what I mean," she said.

We ordered a Lemon Drop to split and, when it was gone, we went up to our room and quickly succumbed to the weariness of surviving a hard day.

CHAPTER TWENTY-TWO

We left Los Angeles the next morning while the moon was still brighter than the sun. It was the best way to beat the traffic and to get me back to the office on time. Monroe was meeting me there at eight.

I walked Marina to her Miata, gave her a quick kiss and told her I'd see her at my place later that night. For a second, I thought she was going to mention our conversation at the bar from the day before but instead she folded herself into the little convertible and started the engine.

I watched until she'd exited the underground parking lot and then climbed into the Camaro and pushed the start button. The rumble of the smooth, powerful engine as it echoed throughout the parking lot was hugely satisfying.

As planned for, the drive home was smooth and without much traffic. The sun rose regally in the East as I took the 101 all the way home, listening to KFI AM 640's Bill Handel rave on about the news for the length of the entire trip. The clock on the dashboard told me it was 7:41 when I pulled into one of the several open parking spaces on California Street, right below my office. It was a rare day when parking like that was available. It was also a rare day that I got to the office before eight.

I had just opened the building's outside door when a horn sounded behind me. I turned to see a sleek Mercedes Benz sedan pulling into the spot next to the Camaro. Mongo glared at me through the windshield from the driver's seat. I gave him a dazzling smile and a cheerful wave. His superpower of indifference seemed to have made him immune to it.

The back door of the Mercedes popped open, and Shale Monroe climbed out. As expected, he wore a pair of tan cargo shorts, what looked like a crisp new black t-shirt and that same pair of sandals from a manufacturer I couldn't identify. Normally, it would have been like looking in a mirror, but I'd come straight from the hotel and still had my travelling clothes on.

"Morning, Brace!" Monroe said, holding out a familiar flat box. "I brought Krispy Kreme."

I closed the door and took the box from Monroe. He thumped the hood of the Mercedes with his knuckles (which I'm sure Mongo wasn't too happy about, not that he'd ever say anything about it) and the big man backed out of the space and disappeared down in the direction of the beach.

I sat down on the curb, opened the box, and felt a smile curl beneath my nose. A dozen original donuts, and they were still warm. I pulled one out and then pushed the box over to Monroe who took one for himself. We sat a moment, chewing the doughy sweetness.

"What's the plan today?" Monroe asked.

"We go back to the Racquet Club."

Monroe looked disappointed. "Really?"

"Really," I told him. "We've got to get some better pictures of the mystery man that was sitting with Mrs. Wilder," I said. "We have to identify him. Once we know who he is, we can start learning more about him."

"Google," Monroe quoted. "The Private Detective's Best Friend."

"And don't you forget it." I took out another donut, offered the box to Monroe, and he took another, too.

"This time we're going out early," I told him. "As soon as we finish these donuts and stop somewhere to get some supplies. Based on our visit the other day, this guy arrived before Mrs. Wilder did."

"That's right," Monroe said, wiping away a crumb of donut from the corner of his mouth. "We saw her arrive. He must have already been inside."

"Exactly," I said. "And he left after she did because we didn't see him when she came out."

"But how do we know he's going to show up today?" Monroe asked.

"We don't," I replied. "It's a crap shoot, emphasis on the crap."

Monroe finished his second donut, declined when I offered him a third. I, myself, offered no such declination.

I carried what was left of the donut dozen (seven, that should get us through the day) to the Camaro and set it on the back seat. Monroe and I climbed in front. I started the engine, carefully checked my rear window, and backed out into California Street. It was a short hop to the freeway, and we were quickly on our way to the Lemon Grove Racquet Club once again.

We stopped at a Circle K for supplies: A six-pack of Coke Zeroes, a couple bags of chips and some Hostess cupcakes. Growing young detectives must keep their bodies well-nourished.

There were only a few cars in the Club's parking lot when we arrived shortly after 8:30 and I was surprised to see a pair of men in crisp new tennis outfits playing on one of the courts, bouncing a bright yellow ball between them. They didn't look like tennis players, they looked like lawyers pretending to be tennis players. They also didn't look comfortable out there on the court but continued the back-and-forth earnestly.

I didn't recognize any of the cars from our previous visit, but I hadn't really done a full inventory last time, so anything was possible. I asked Monroe if any looked familiar to him and he shook his head, no. I reached into the back, grabbed another donut (was disappointed that they were no longer warm) and washed down a bite with the Coke Zero.

"How'd you ever get into this business?" Monroe asked. I had offered him a donut a few minutes earlier and he had declined once again. The man was starting to disappoint me.

"Can't really say," I told him. "Kinda fell into it, truth be told. I took what I thought was going to be a summer job from a private detective in town and ended up spending almost five years there. When he retired, I struck out on my own." I laughed. "That guy, Augustus Teague—Gus—loves to tell people that he taught me everything I know. But you know what? He did. If it wasn't for Gus, I'd be working security at the mall or something."

"Augustus Teague," Monroe said, feeling the name in his mouth. "I might steal that name for my movie."

"You might want to clear that with Gus, first," I said. "Guy's in his early 70s now and he could still kick both of our asses."

Monroe laughed. He didn't know how serious I was.

A shiny late model Ford Mustang pulled into the lot, and we were both silent as we watched with rapt attention. The man who climbed out of the Mustang, however, bore no resemblance to our man of interest.

"What about you?" I asked Monroe. "How'd you end up in the movie business?"

Monroe smiled. "Like everyone else in showbiz," he said. "Family business. My grandad produced movies, my mom and dad produced movies and it just seemed natural to me."

"Not everyone wants to follow in their parents' footsteps."

"It's all I ever wanted to do," Monroe said. "The Glitz, the glamour. The money. It's everything they say it is."

"I've heard it's a hard business."

"I never said it was easy," Monroe confirmed. "There are times when I wish I'd gone to dentist school instead of getting into showbiz. The politics, the lawsuits, the jerk-off studio trolls, the superstar prima donnas. Sometimes you just want to put your head in an oven." He smiled. "But other times are nothing short of glorious. Going to a premiere of a movie *you* made. Winning an award, any type of award." He looked at me sharply. "Don't let them tell you that the Oscar is the only one that matters. I'd give my left kidney for any award. As long as the trophy is nice, and my name is engraved on the front."

I laughed.

Monroe gave me a look. "You ever thought about working in the movies? You've got those rugged old school good looks and build," he said. "Won't ever be a leading man, but you could be a hell of a character actor. You know, like Jonathan Banks."

This time I guffawed. "That'll be the day."

An ancient but well-kept Rolls Royce entered the parking lot and I admired it as it passed. There wasn't a dent or a scratch anywhere on it and, if it wasn't for the fact that it was obviously designed and built in another age, you could have sworn it was brand new. They were probably one of the least practical vehicles ever made, but Rolls Royce just shouted class and wealth and they were well-built machines on top of that.

"That's him," Monroe said, sitting forward with a snap. "That's the guy."

My eyebrows furrowed. "That car wasn't here yesterday. I would have remembered it."

"You think a guy who can afford that car only has one?"

He had a point. We watched as the Rolls slid into the parking slot nearest the Club's main door and its sole occupant got out.

He was a tall, thin man, probably in his late 60s, and he was dressed exactly as you'd imagine a rich, retired man would dress for the Racquet Club. He wore a pair of snow-white tennis shoes that looked from this distance like they were brand new. A pair of white tennis socks rose out of the shoes and clung to his legs at about mid-shin. Keeping the white motif, his tennis shorts were white, too, and looked like the kind of designer quality that promoted fashion over function. His powder blue shirt also looked fresh out of the box and was adorned over the heart with a stylized W, which I recognized as the Wilson tennis company logo.

He kind of reminded me of Ted Knight in *Caddyshack* except that, where Ted's hair had also been snow-white, this guy's was dark gray and matched his pencil-thin mustache perfectly. Too perfectly, in fact, to be anything but salon-bought and paid for.

I lifted my iPhone and started snapping pictures. Zoomed in. Zoomed out. Took bursts. No matter what else happened, I wasn't going to end up with photos as useless as those Monroe had taken a few days ago.

Suddenly, the dome light came to life as Monroe opened the passenger door and stepped out into the parking lot. "Hey, what ..." was all I managed before the door slammed shut again.

I watched as Monroe jogged toward the man at a gallop. He called out to him. The man turned. I couldn't hear what they were saying, but they had a short conversation. It ended with a hardy handshake and the exchange of what I assumed were business cards. The man took one quick glance in my direction, and then continued into the building as Monroe came bouncing back to the Camaro, the shit-eating grin I'd seen before once again plastered across his face.

"His name is Rutherford Archambault," Monroe said, slipping back into the Camaro and passing me a business card. "He's been a member here for sixteen years. He highly recommends the Veal Bolognese in the restaurant and told me that, if I needed a sponsor for membership, he'd be more than willing."

I laughed, a little. "You told him who you were."

"Damn right," Monroe said, beaming. "And that I was considering becoming a member. He also offered me his accounting services."

I glanced at the card. RUTHERFORD ARCHAM-BAULT, it declared. CERTIFIED PUBLIC ACCOUNT.

I looked up over the dash at the silver Rolls Royce parked near the Club entrance.

"Another accountant," I said. "Just like Mr. Wilder."

Monroe wiggled his eyebrows. "Ooh. The plot thickens."

"Maybe," I admitted. "But who knew accountants made enough money to afford Rolls Royces?"

"Or ridiculous membership fees at a shitty club."

I looked around. "Doesn't seem too shitty," I said.

"I was making a point."

I tossed the business card on the dash, took a sip of Coke Zero and grabbed yet another donut. That was probably two too many, but I promised myself I'd work extra hard at the gym tonight. "Don't bring these next time," I told Monroe.

"You know, my accountant gets about $350 an hour," Monroe said. "And I'm not his only client. Pretty sure that fucker could afford a Rolls Royce."

"My accountant gets $250 a year," I told him. "In April, when he does my taxes."

While Monroe kept an eye on the parking lot entrance, eyes peeled for any sign of Mrs. Wilder, I thought about what to do next. We could sit here and wait for Mrs. Wilder to arrive but, unless she came out of the building with Rutherford Archambault and headed for the local Motel 6, that might be a waste of time. Monroe's faux membership tricks would only work so many times and we sure didn't need Mrs. Wilder or Archambault getting used to seeing our faces.

Or we could head back to the office and Google "Rutherford Archambault" until our fingers bled. But it was the same story there; all that research might lead to nothing. Google was the private detective's best friend, but she could also be stubbornly fickle.

I briefly considered using my iPhone to do the research work while we waited for Mrs. Wilder, thus killing two birds with one stone. But I absolutely hated typing on the phone. My fat thumbs came up with words that mother nature had never intended and spell check only made things worse. A simple word like "day" could come out like "Mephistopheles."

But anything was better than sitting there and waffling over what the next step was.

"Let's go back to the office," I told Monroe. "And see what we can find out about Mr. Archambault. Worse comes to worse we can come back out here tomorrow and do this all over again."

"I'm really sick of sitting here in this parking lot," Monroe said.

"Yeah," I agreed. "That makes two of us."

Chapter Twenty-Three

It took a couple of hours, but this was what we learned:

Rutherford Archambault was born in 1953. He was raised in the city of Covina, California where he went to the aptly named Covina Elementary School and the equally aptly named Covina High School (Go, Colts!). He graduated in 1970 and immediately attended college at California Lutheran University (which I was happy to learn was not named Covina College). Four years later, he earned his bachelor's degree and immediately went to work for his father's accounting firm in Los Angeles.

In 1979, Archambault left his father's firm and, with Joshua Cander, his "longtime friend" (according to their company bio), formed Arhcambault/Cander Accounting.

The company grew at a very successful rate until, in 2009, when Archambault and Cander sold the company to H&R Block and they both retired. Based on his recent conversation with Monroe, Archambault still did some work on the side.

Archambault was fond of Irish Setters, expensive cars (i.e., Rolls Royce) and action/adventure movies. His favorite was *Raiders of the Lost Ark*. He divorced his first wife, Naomi, in 1978 and married his current wife, Libby (short for Elisabeth) in 1980. The couple apparently didn't see much of each other, and often took separate vacations; Archambault vacationing in Las Vegas while his wife preferred the white sand beaches of Cabo, Mexico.

He had never been arrested and, surprisingly, had only been sued twice throughout his illustrious career. I would have thought that the accounting business would have been somewhat more litigious.

He had no children with either of his wives and apparently had never intended to reproduce. "That's why I don't have kids," he once posted on Facebook. "I've got enough to worry about. Me!"

Monroe and I sat in my office, thumbing through the printouts we'd made of our research. We were both silent, reading and re-reading. An empty to-go bag from Finney's Crafthouse downstairs sat crookedly on my desk. It had once held Nashville Hot Chicken Sliders, a Thai Steak salad, and an onion ring tower. It now held nothing. The remnants of our meal were scattered across my desk, amidst which were two dangerously close-to-empty bottles of Lagunitas IPA.

I pushed away the stack of papers in front of me and looked at Monroe. "So," I said. "What have we learned here?"

"At first blush," Monroe said. "I'd have to say not a goddamn thing."

"And you would be correct," I said. "Which begs the question: Is there nothing to learn?"

Monroe looked at me curiously.

"Maybe we're barking up the wrong tree." I clarified.

"Maybe we're not," Monroe said. "I mean, it's not like some webpage is gonna say, 'Rutherford Archambault loves Irish Setters and fucking other people's wives.'"

"Probably not."

"So maybe we're barking up the right tree," Monroe said. "But we're barking at the wrong *branch*."

I pursed my lips and nodded. "That's some deep shit," I said.

Monroe laughed. "So, what do we do next?"

"You ask that a lot."

"It's the right question," Monroe said. "I mean, it seems like we haven't covered a lot of ground here."

"That's because we haven't."

"Once again, I ask: What's the next step?"

I stared across the mess of my desk at him and thought for a second. "You know what?" I said. "Let me sleep on it. You may be right. We may be taking the wrong tack. Let me muse over it and we'll talk about it in the morning."

"Eight o'clock?"

"That'll work."

"I'll text Mongo."

While his fingers danced across his phone (he was apparently much better at typing on that small screen than I was) I thought carefully about what he'd just said. What *was* the next step? I was already sick of staking out parking lots and hoping to catch forbidden lovers in the act. And Google, despite being my best friend, had proved virtually fruitless this past week.

I decided I'd do just what I told Monroe I'd do. Sleep on it. See if I couldn't come up with a fresh start in the morning.

But first, I had some more staking out to do. This time at Cassandra's place out on the Avenue.

CHAPTER TWENTY-FOUR

Both Cassandra and her new beau were home when I pulled up across the street and killed the Camry's engine. Well, at least their cars were there, parked in the driveway in the exact same configuration as they were the last time I paid them a visit.

I parked in my usual space, one house down, across the street, and hoped that the neighbors wouldn't get suspicious. It's hard to do a stakeout in a quiet neighborhood because everyone knows everyone. They may not be best friends, but they see each other coming and going all the time. Unrecognized vehicles stand out, even something as non-descript as my boring, beige Camry. So far, though, so good.

Marina had guilted me into eating healthier so instead of the usual bag of hot dogs, there was a paper-wrapped tuna sandwich from Jersey Mike's on the passenger seat. It could be argued whether a tuna sandwich was indeed healthier than three hot dogs (especially when I had ordered the Giant), but at least the sandwich had greens.

I got myself settled and picked up the book I'd been reading. *The Law of Innocence* by Michael Connelly, another Lincoln Lawyer novel. I'd read no more than half a page when my cell phone rang. It was Lt. Steven Powell of the Ventura Police Department returning my call.

"Steve, thanks for calling."

"What's up, Heller?

"More of the same. Out detecting."

"Probably what a detective should do."

"Hey, listen, I need a favor …"

"Of course, you do."

"Actually, it's not for me. It's for Marina."

"Oh?" Steve asked, his tone changing. "Everything okay?"

"Everything is not okay," I said. "Her mother passed away last week."

"Jesus. I'm sorry. I hadn't heard."

"Yeah, thanks," I said. "She's taking it pretty hard."

"Parents are tough," Powell said. "Lost both of mine within weeks of each other."

"Sorry to hear that."

"Yeah, it was brutal. How about you?"

"Me? I'm a lucky man. Both of my parents are still alive. And doing well."

"You *are* a lucky man. Enjoy them while you can."

"Listen, about that favor …" I paused. Wondered how to make the request not sound weird.

"Go on," Powell prompted.

"It's about Millicent."

"Millicent?" Powell said. "Oh, you mean Millie? The psychic?" The last word became a whisper and I realized he was probably still at the station. Police departments all over the country use psychics on a regular basis but they don't like to admit it. Or even talk about it out loud.

"Yeah, that one," I said.

"What about her?"

"Marina wants to meet her," I said. "Wants to talk to her."

Powell was silent for a moment. "Why does she want to do that?"

"Something about her mother."

"Who just died."

"Yes."

Powell took a breath. "She knows that Millie's not one of those carnival psychics, right? She doesn't hold seances or talk to the dead."

"She knows," I said. "I told her."

"Then I don't understand."

"Neither do I," I said.

I could hear the squeak of his office chair as he squirmed on the other end. "Do you think this is a good idea?"

"I do not."

"I'm with you," Powell said. "I could say no."

"Part of me wishes you will," I said. "Part of me hopes you won't."

"That's not very fucking helpful."

"I know."

Powell let out a long breath. "All right, I'll give her a call. Get back to you in the next day or so."

"Maybe by then," I said. "Marina will have changed her mind."

"Let's hope so. Talk to you then."

"Thanks," I said. "Bye."

The night had become too dark to read without the dome light on, and the dome light was a beacon that told the entire neighborhood there was an interloper present. So, I sat in the dark, listening to a podcast about the Zodiac Killer. For an unsolved crime, that case had been solved about a thousand times and each time with a different solution.

My tuna sandwich was about half gone when I heard raised voices and, a moment later, a door slammed so loudly it sounded like a gunshot. In fact, I'm sure half of the people on the block were snatching up their cell phones and typing "Did someone just hear a gunshot?" into their Nextdoor apps.

I saw movement in the driveway of Cassandra's place and suddenly she was there, stomping away from the house furiously. The door slammed again, and she turned, raising her hand, finger pointed in anger.

"No! No!" She barked. "You stay the fuck in there! I've got nothing to say to you!" She was wearing a pair of grey sweatpants and a LAKERS t-shirt that was at least two sizes too big for her. Her feet were bare. She marched over to her car, tried the door handle and then smacked the window with the side of her hand. Apparently, she had left her keys inside.

Locke appeared, walking toward her, his hands up and open in a questioning manner. "Where you gonna go?" he asked in a normal tone of voice, and with an expression that said he was the most patient man in the world. He wore a pair of flashy red basketball shorts and a plain white t-shirt.

"Fucking *anywhere!*" Cassandra spat, stepping back. "Fucking anywhere *you're* not!"

"Don't be like that," he said. "Come back inside."

"I'm not going to do it," Cassandra said. "I'm not going to be your fucking maid." Her volume level had diminished, and she'd stopped walking. The gap between the two of them closed. "I'm sick of this shit."

"I told you I'd clean it up," he said in a voice so low I almost couldn't catch the words. "Now come back *inside.*"

He spat out the last word and lashed out with his left hand to snatch at her right wrist. She tried to pull back, but he held tight, twisting, and her wrist went the wrong way. Cassandra gave out a little mewl of pain.

I was up and out of the car, but the dome light betrayed me. Locke's head snapped in my direction, and he let go of Cassandra's wrist. She gripped it with her other hand, glanced my way, and then ran into the house. I didn't think she recognized me in the shadows.

Locke stood where he was, glaring at me with venom. "The fuck you looking at?" he growled, before turning and going back into the house.

I didn't get the chance to tell him, but I knew exactly what I was looking at.

A dead man.

CHAPTER TWENTY-FIVE

In what was becoming a painfully boring routine, I found Monroe and his pal Mongo sitting on the bench in front of my office when I arrived at 8:02 AM. Mongo and I did our daily dance of indifference and, as Mongo disappeared down the hall, Monroe and I stepped into my office and took our places.

"You didn't bring donuts," I said.

"You told me not to."

"I was wrong," I said. "So, before you ask what's on today's agenda, it's a field trip day."

"Good," he said. "Better than sitting in that boring ass parking lot all day."

"Maybe. Maybe not."

Monroe gave me a look.

"We're going to tail Mrs. Wilder," I told him. "All day. Wherever she goes, we go."

Monroe nodded. "Okay by me. It's still better than sitting around waiting in that parking lot all day."

"Still gonna be a lot of waiting," I told him. "She goes to the hairdresser; we go to the hairdresser. She's getting her hair done, we're out in the car until she's through. She goes to the movies, we're in the car until her movie's over. She goes to the grocery store; we wait outside until she comes out."

"You know," Monroe said. "This detective gig kinda sucks."

I laughed. "You aren't wrong about that, my friend."

The outer office door opened, and someone walked in. I quickly glanced down, made sure I was presentable, and pointed Monroe in the direction of the chair in the corner near the coat rack.

Instead of the expected knock, however, the inner office door burst open, and a man strode in. Today, he was dressed in a business suit, but I recognized him immediately from his pencil-thin mustache.

Rutherford Archambault.

His red face and clenched fists told me he wasn't there for a consultation. He glared first at me, then at Monroe sitting in the corner, and then quickly looked around the office.

"Okay," he said. "Who the fuck are you guys?"

I smiled brightly. "I'm Bartles and he's Jaymes," I said. "Can I interest you in a wine cooler?"

Archambault blanched and, if possible, his face went redder. He took a threatening step toward my desk. "I didn't come here for any lip," he said, spittle spraying. "I wanna know who you are and what you're up to."

"My name's on the door," I said, pointing. "Maybe next time come in a little more tranquil and read it before you ask."

His eyes squeezed tight. "I told you, I'm not gonna take any of your shit …"

"Then don't come bursting into my office screaming at me," I said, standing. Archambault was tall but I was taller. He was thin, and I had some weight on me. Most of it was muscle. Some of it was Del Taco.

For a moment, I didn't think that was going to matter. Archambault leaned forward as though he intended to move in on me but then suddenly rocked back on his heels, taking a deep breath.

"Why don't you sit down, and we can talk about this," I said. "Like civilized human beings."

Archambault started to argue and then quickly changed his mind. He dropped into the client chair across from my desk and stared up at me expectantly. I glanced over at Monroe to see him huddled in the corner, eyes as wide as saucers. The threat of near violence had scared him. Good.

"Are you gonna tell me who you are and what you've been doing at the Club?" Archambault asked. "Or do I have to take this to the next level?"

I smirked. "Jesus, give it a rest already," I said. "We're all adults here, we can talk without the toothless threats."

"You'll see if they're toothless," he growled.

I shook my head. Archambault in a business suit was only two degrees scarier than Archambault in his silly tennis outfit.

"Okay," I said, smiling warmly. "My name is Brace Heller, and I'm a private detective."

Archambault seemed surprised.

"You would have known that," I said, "If you'd taken the time to read the name on the door."

He snarled and hooked his head in Monroe's direction. "Who's he?"

"That is Shale Monroe," I told him. "The Hollywood producer."

"You expect me to believe that?"

I shook my head and shrugged. "I don't really care what you believe, Mr. Archambault. It's the truth and you can take it or leave it."

He shot a glance at Monroe and then turned back to me. "How do you know me?"

"You gave Mr. Monroe your card."

"Under false pretenses!"

"Maybe," I said. "Maybe not. He still may want to become a member of the Lemon Grove Racquet Club."

Out of the corner of my eye, I saw Monroe slowly shake his head and mouth the word "no."

Archambault, still glaring at me, said, "Not if I have anything to do with it."

"I guess that means you're withdrawing your promise to endorse him."

The red face came back. "Goddammit, boy, you better stop toying with me," he said.

I spread my palms in a gesture of friendship. "Okay," I said. "You know who we are, you know what we do. What else do you want to know?"

"What were you doing at the Club?"

"Research."

"What kind of research?"

"I can't tell you that," I said. "It's confidential. Client privilege."

"Bullshit."

"Take it up with the State of California," I said.

"Does it have to do with me?"

"Can't tell you."

"Is it about the Club?"

"Can't say."

"Well, what can you say?" Archambault said, face reddening again.

"Not much," I told him. "Sorry."

"Fuck your sorry," Archambault spat, and his face puffed up in the color of a radish. "Whatever you're up to, it ends now. Do you hear me? You stop today. This minute."

I sat quietly and watched him for a moment. "Or what?"

He leapt to his feet and backhanded the telephone off my desk. It clattered to the ground with a jarring *brrrrinnng.* I heard Monroe utter a soft moan in the corner.

"Or you'll fucking see!" Archambault screamed, pushing his swollen blood-red face closer to mine. "You'll just fucking see!" He banged his fist so hard on the desktop that my monitor jumped up and down. And then—with the resounding slam of not one but two doors—he was gone.

The room was silent for a moment. Finally, I got out of my chair and picked the phone up off the floor. It was a goner. The receiver had broken at the mouthpiece and the numbers seven and nine were missing from the dial pad. I dropped it into the wastebasket.

Monroe sat wide-eyed in the corner, staring worriedly at me. I gave him a wan smile.

"Change of plans," I said.

He blinked. "What do you mean?"

"We're gonna follow *that* guy," I said.

CHAPTER TWENTY-SIX

I was hoping Archambault had driven the Rolls Royce rather than whatever other car he had in his garage and luck was with me. As Monroe and I came out of the building, the Rolls was turning right from California onto Main Street. The Rolls would be light years easier to tail than any other car, especially because we didn't know what other cars Archambault might own.

"Get in," I said to Monroe, and we both climbed into the Camry. I was glad we had the Camry today instead of the Camaro. People pay much less attention to a non-descript family car than a bitchin' muscle car.

I backed out too quickly, earning the angry blast of a horn as I entered the lane, and got another toot as I pulled a U-turn in the middle of the street and headed back up California. Following Archambault's path, I coasted through the red light and turned right onto Main Street.

"Can you see him?" Monroe said, stretching his neck to see up the road.

"No," I said. "But he's there. And he'll be easy to find."

I blew the next light at Chestnut and caught a glimpse of the Rolls as it turned left on N. Ash. "Got him," I said.

We got to Ash just in time to see the Rolls turn right onto Poli.

"Poli's a thoroughfare," I told Monroe. "He'll probably stay on it for some time."

We turned onto Ash, and I raced up to Poli Street. The traffic was light, and we were back behind the Rolls in a matter of seconds. There were three cars between us, and we kept back far enough so that Archambault wouldn't see us. Not that he would make us. He'd only ever seen the Camaro at the Club (unless he'd been parked outside, waiting for me to arrive at the office that morning) and we were far enough back he couldn't see our faces. Plus, he was such a hothead, he probably never even considered we might be following him.

As I'd predicted, Archambault kept the Rolls heading east on Poli until it became Foothill Road somewhere around Grove Street. There were sometimes three cars between us, sometimes as many as five. The Rolls stood out like a golden sore thumb. We could see it clearly as we followed.

We passed the Ventura Medical Center on our right and Arroyo Verde Park on our left. Still, Archambault kept the Rolls Royce on Foothill. I wondered if he was just heading home. If so, we'd learn nothing. We already had his address from our internet search. I was hoping for something just a little more salacious.

He wasn't going home. The left taillight of the Rolls began flashing and Archambault pulled the massive automobile into a turn lane. The flow of oncoming traffic forced him to sit there for a moment, waiting for the road to clear, and I had no choice but to drive past him. I watched in the rearview mirror as the Rolls turned and headed up a street that led into the hills, then took my next left into a church parking lot, spun a U-turn and headed back the way we came.

I turned right on the street that the Rolls had taken, Cobblestone Drive, and followed it into the hills. We found ourselves in a cul-de-sac. Massive, beautiful homes towered over us. The homes on our right were stunning, modern dwellings that probably went for more money than I'd made in my lifetime, and almost as much money than Monroe had made on his last picture. But it was the homes on the left that were the real deal. These modern two- and three-story homes were just as big and classy as the others, but clung to the edge of a mountainside, offering a view of the Pacific Ocean that would draw gasps of awe and disbelief from even the most dispassionate viewer.

As I rounded the corner, I caught sight of the Rolls, now facing us, parked in front of one of those houses.

"There he is," Monroe said, unnecessarily.

I pulled over and brought the Camry to a stop, killed the engine. "Roll down your window," I said to Monroe, as I did so myself.

At first there was no sign of Archambault. He wasn't in the Rolls, and he wasn't anywhere out in the open. Had he gone into one of those homes? If so, which one? It wasn't *his* place. I knew that he lived out near the Harbor. Who lived here that Archambault could have come to see?

"You hear that?" Monroe said.

I shook my head, cocked it, and concentrated on listening.

There it was. Someone banging on a door. Loudly. The noise traveling from somewhere up near where the Rolls was parked.

"Come on!" I heard someone screaming. "I know you're in there! Open the goddamn door!" It was Archambault. I recognized his bold, stringent voice.

The pounding continued. "Don't do this! Talk to me!" he yelled again. We couldn't see him, but I thought I could place him from the location of his voice. He was either at the house directly in front of where the Rolls was parked, or he was one house down.

"Fine! Fuck it!" Archambault yelled, giving the door one more furious pounding. "And fuck you!"

And he came striding angrily down the driveway of the home nearest the end of the cul-de-sac, glaring over his shoulders as if daring the person inside the home to open the door and confront him. He walked to the driver's side of the Rolls, flipped the bird to anyone in the house who might have been watching, and then climbed in. The Rolls' big engine roared to life, and it began to move.

"Down!" I said to Monroe. We both dipped into our seats as the Rolls roared by. I figured Archambault was too caught up in his anger to pay any attention to a car parked on the side of the road but better safe than sorry.

After a moment, we both sat slowly back up.

"What the hell was that about?" Monroe said.

"Search me," I said. "But we did learn something."

"Oh, yeah?" Monroe said. "What's that?"

"Rutherford Archambault should probably invest in some anger management courses."

I started the Camry and we drove the end of the cul-de-sac and turned around. As we passed the house that Archambault had been screaming at, I stopped and pointed to the mailbox on the street out front.

It was decorated to look like a birdhouse, painted a soft blue with images of delicate flowers and shrubbery brightening it. A fake circular hole was painted in the door, I guess where the birds would have gone in had it been real. It reminded me of the portable hole that Bugs Bunny and Roger Rabbit used.

But what really interested me was the name plate on the side of the mailbox.

It read: WILDER.

CHAPTER TWENTY-SEVEN

Marina surprised me by saying yes to Monroe's party. "I'm not in a festive mood," she declared. "But I am curious. I've never been to a big Hollywood party."

The party wasn't in Hollywood, however, but rather the city of Calabasas, located in the south-western portion of the San Fernando Valley. I'd heard that a lot of celebrities lived there, the city being just close enough to the studios to be convenient but far enough to get away from it all. It was about an hour's drive from my place in Ventura on a good day but, on a Friday, traffic added at least twenty minutes of travel time.

Following the map and directions on the invite Monroe had given me, it wasn't difficult to find his home. We were in a quaint yet affluent neighborhood and Monroe's street was lined with parked cars on either side. If there was any further question where the party was, the answer was found in the two tuxedo-clad guards standing at the front gate of a home near the middle of the street. They stood there at attention, unnecessary sunglasses firmly in place, and compared names to clipboards before allowing people to pass inside.

The buzz of voices, laughter and music was also a clue.

I parked on the corner at the end of the street and Marina and I climbed out of the Camaro and walked back to the house. Marina was gorgeous in her black party dress and high heels, and I was dressed to a T in the Brooks Brothers suit Marina had picked out for me because I was a fashion idiot.

We couldn't see much of the home as we approached due to an enormous hedge that blocked the view from the street. "Heller," I said to the guard on the right as we walked up to the gate. His bald head glistened with perspiration in the warm evening air, and I couldn't blame him. The tuxedo he wore looked stifling as hell. That's why I was known as the Shorts and Sandals Detective and not the Brooks Brothers Madison Fit Stretch Wool Two-Button 1818 Suit Detective.

"You're good," the guard said, putting a ball-point checkmark by our name on the list. "Enjoy."

We stepped through the gate and found ourselves in a spacious front yard. Two groups of three white tables were scattered across the grass at regular intervals, each table protected from an unlikely rainstorm by a white umbrella mushrooming out of a hole in its middle. A stone path stretched between them. Curiously, no one sat at the tables, although there were about fifteen people standing around, sipping on liquids of various colors and shades in highball glasses or stemware.

Yacht rock pulsed playfully from hidden speakers that seemed to be in every corner of the yard. The dulcet tones of Christopher Cross sifted through the air.

"Not quite the mansion I was expecting," I said quietly to Marina, nodding in the direction of the house.

"Shush," she told me.

It was a single-story unit, admittedly much longer than my place and Marina's laid end-to-end. I believe realtors call it "ranch-style." The garage was on the left and connected to the house near a front porch that looked cozy and rarely used. A pair of wooden steps led up to the porch and the front door. To the right of the front door, it appeared that an addition had been built, slightly taller than the rest of the house, but equal in size. The windows were crisscrossed with metal bars that I think were more for decorative purposes than protection and at the opposite end was another front door, this one with a front-gabled room to its right.

"I think it's cute," Marina said, taking it in.

I laughed. "That's the thing," I said. "It is cute. But I expected something bigger. More Beverly Hills."

There was a bar just beyond the tables, so Marina and I threaded our way through the other guests and got in line. The servers were quick and efficient, and it didn't take long for our turn.

"Whiskey," I said, "And she'll have a Chardonnay."

"Mojitos only," said the server, smiling brightly. "Whiskey and Chardonnay at the bar inside."

"Okay," I said with a shrug. "Two mojitos, then."

While we waited for our mojitos to be poured, I turned away from the bar and scanned the faces of the other guests. This was a Hollywood party (in Calabasas). Surely, there'd be someone I recognized from the movies. Or TV. Or Music.

There was not.

"You see anyone you recognize?" I asked Marina when our drinks were ready, and I had passed hers over.

"I do not," she said. "And I've been looking."

The mojitos were delicious. Marina and I agreed that they may have been the best we've ever had. We wandered around, drinks in hand, offering smiles and nodding greetings to strangers as we passed. Everyone was in groups of four or five and, within those groups at least, they seemed to know one another well. Their conversations seemed bright and energetic.

"Let's see if we can find Monroe," I suggested.

We stepped up onto the porch and said a brief hello to the small group gathered there. They returned our greeting politely and continued with their conversation, part of which I understood to be a discussion of whether Martin Scorsese's *The Irishman* deserved at least one Oscar and that it was a crime that it in fact won bupkis.

There were more people inside than out, and Marina and I found ourselves threading through the crowd with turned shoulders and lots of "Excuse Me's." Everyone had a drink in their hand and their voices were raised in conversation.

We found the inside bar and I got my whiskey (Nob Hill) and Marina got her chardonnay. I wasn't sure which winery it came from, but I assumed it wasn't Two Buck Chuck. This may not have been Beverly Hills, but it was a Hollywood party, after all.

After a few moments of pushing through the throng, we found a relatively open space near the kitchen and hovered, enjoying our drinks.

Marina tapped my arm. "There," she said, nodding toward the corner. "You know that guy. From that cop show, *Atlanta Arms*."

I turned my head in the direction she had indicated and, in fact, did recognize the guy.

"I think you're right," I said. "Hard to tell seeing him in street clothes."

"And there," Marina said, nodding to her left. "I think that's Reggie Blue."

I looked over and there was no mistaking it. Blue was one of those veteran rock stars who should have known better than to dress the way he did, especially at his age. He looked like a drunken pirate in a pair of black tights and a gothic jacket with buttons the size of doubloons. But what did I know? Blue still made millions of dollars every year. I drove a 2013 Toyota Camry.

"Brace Heller!" came the voice of Shale Monroe. "I'm so glad you made it!" I looked over to see Monroe heading straight for us, the massive shadow of Mongo just behind him. Monroe was wearing what looked like a vintage tailcoat and tuxedo. I was surprised there was no top hat.

Mongo was in his usual black suit. They came over and Monroe pulled me into a bear hug, pounded my back with a series of hearty slaps, then pushed away and turned his attention to Marina.

"And you must be Marina," he said, lifting her hand and kissing her fingers. "Brace has told me so much about you."

Marina glanced over at me and I shook my head. *No, I haven't.*

"I was so sorry to hear about your mother," Monroe said, picking up Marina's hand again. "I lost my mother just about five years ago," he added. "There's nothing quite so hard."

"Thank you," Marina managed.

"Okay! You got your drinks, you've mingled, I hope." Monroe winked at me. "You have mingled, haven't you, Brace? Marina?"

We nodded.

"Then have fun! Enjoy! The food truck should be arriving shortly. The best tacos in Los Angeles."

"Thanks for having us," I said.

But Monroe was already gone, heading off in the opposite direction, already waving someone else down.

Mongo gave me a quick bleak look and followed him.

"You want to wait for tacos?" I asked Marina. "The best in Los Angeles."

"I think I'd rather have In-N-Out," she said.

"I love the way you think," I told her. "Let's blow this joint."

A short time later, we sat in the In-N-Out parking lot, Marina working on her hamburger (no onions, add pickles) and me on my Double Double (extra cheese, no onion, no tomato, add pickles).

"Well, that was weird," I said.

Marina nibbled for a moment and said, "Yes, it was."

"Not what I expected," I said. "I mean, it was a nice party, and it was probably pretty expensive."

"Best tacos in Los Angeles," Marina laughed.

"But it wasn't what I expected."

"What did you expect?"

"Well, you know," I said. "Like you see in the movies. A big mansion, three stories at least. Big Roman columns holding up the front roof. Movie stars you recognize like that …" I snapped my fingers. "… strolling around, talking about how their weekends were. People in tuxedoes drinking martinis and discussing their next film." I shrugged. "Maybe even a showbiz gossip columnist flitting around, taking notes and stealing secrets."

Marina laughed. "That's the problem," she said. "That's what you see in the movies. It's not real life."

"I guess not," I said. "Did you hear that guy standing next to us just before we left?"

Marina shook her head.

"I think he was telling that girl he was with that there was a room in the back that was designated just for sex."

Marina sputtered, almost spitting out some Diet Coke. "No!"

"I'm serious. He said there was even a sign on it. SEX ROOM, or something like that."

"We should have checked it out," Marina said.

"No way. I'm not having sex in a SEX ROOM whether the sign says that or not."

Marina punched me on the shoulder. "No, silly," she said. "We should have just checked it out."

"Got a photo or something?"

"Yes!"

"Post it on the 'gram?"

Marina laughed.

We finished our meals, gathered up our trash and dumped it in the barrel near the restaurants' trademark crossed palms.

"Ready to go?" I asked her.

"I am," she said. "Brace?"

"Yeah, honey?"

"Thank you. I had a good time tonight."

I gave her a quick kiss on the lips. "Good," I said. "I'm glad."

We climbed back into the Camaro and headed up the 101 North toward home.

Chapter Twenty-Eight

It was Saturday night, and we had watched a really bad movie on Netflix that made us both wish we had the 98 minutes back that we'd lost. It was my fault, really. Marina had been willing to turn it off after fifteen minutes, but I have a code. Once I start watching something, I watch it until the end. Who knows? Maybe it'll get better.

It almost never does.

We sat side-by-side on the sofa, a blanket warming our laps, Wurzel nested between Marina's left hip and the sofa arm. He'd slept through most of the movie but of course that's what he was born to do: Eat, poop, sleep. Nowhere in the dog owner's manual did it say that dogs would watch movies with you.

Marina sipped chardonnay from a tall, slim glass that was probably designed for champagne while I drank beer out of a June Lake Brewing stainless steel cup. The beer inside the cup was a Tri-Fin Tripel from Leashless Brewing and I felt a little like a traitor drinking it from another brewery's vessel.

Marina was fascinated when I told her about Archambault's loud visit to the Wilder home.

"So do you think he was there to confront Mrs. Wilder?" she asked. "Or Mr. Wilder?"

"That is a valid question," I responded. "To which I have no answer."

"But it could be either."

"Could be," I said. "Although I'm leaning toward Mrs. Wilder considering that Monroe witnessed their lunch together."

"But a lunch doesn't mean an affair."

"It does not."

"Maybe it's a lover's triangle," Marina said. "Maybe Archambault and Mrs. Wilder *are* having an affair. Maybe Archambault wants more than that. Maybe Mr. Wilder is aware of it and the two men are bumping heads. You know, like moose fighting over a mate."

I pursed my lips. "Isn't the plural of 'moose' something like 'meese.'"

"I don't think so."

"Can't be just 'moose.'"

"I think it is."

"Well, whatever it is, we've got some friction," I said. "Archambault is obviously engaged with one of the Wilders, whether it's the Mr. or the Mrs."

"Maybe it has nothing to do with Mrs. Wilder," Marina suggested. "Maybe they're just bumping heads because they're both accountants. Fighting over a client or something."

"Anything's possible."

"So, what are you going to do?"

"Keep watching," I said. "Observe. See where things take us."

"Doesn't sound like much."

"That's because it's not. I've got to gather more information and that's the only way to do it."

"You mean like with Cassandra?"

I nodded. "What I saw this week leads me to believe that Locke may be the abuser Puño was afraid he'd be. But I haven't seen him hit her. And her reaction was understandably upset but she didn't seem to be in distress."

"It was still assault," Marina said tightly.

"You're absolutely right," I said. "But I know what's going to happen to that guy if he's beating her. If he is, then he'll get what he deserves. But I have to be sure."

"Why don't you just ask Cassandra?"

"I can't do that," I said. "You know that. How many of your clients admit to having been abused when you ask them?

Marina nodded slowly. "Some," she said. "Not enough."

"And Cassandra already used the classic answer. She told Puño she fell down."

"Well, you just can't let her stay there and get beaten."

"It really isn't up to me," I said. "I don't have that power. She does. And, unfortunately, Locke does, if Cassandra is too afraid to leave."

"It just sucks," Marina said.

"It absolutely does."

We were quiet for a moment, Marina draining her chardonnay and me gulping my beer.

"Have you heard anything from Steve?"

I took a deep breath. "I have. He spoke to Millicent, and she invited us over on Tuesday afternoon."

"Why didn't you say something earlier?"

"I thought maybe you'd changed your mind."

Marina shook her head solemnly. "I'm not going to change my mind."

"Okay," I said. "I understand. We'll head over there about three, will that work?"

Marina nodded but said nothing. She sat there for a few moments, staring at the blank TV screen, and holding her empty wine glass.

"I'm going to bed," she said after a moment, pulling back the blanket and walking down the hall to the bedroom.

Wurzel rolled over and looked at me with questioning eyes. *What the hell was that all about?* In a second, he was sound asleep again.

"I don't know, boy," I told him. "I just don't know."

CHAPTER TWENTY-NINE

I was already at my desk on Monday morning when Monroe and Mongo showed up at the office. Mongo escorted Monroe as far as the outer door and then turned around and headed back the other way. It saddened me that we would miss our daily ritual of pretending to dislike one another.

"Morning, gumshoe!" Monroe said. He threw a leg over a client chair and plopped down.

I laughed. "Somebody's been reading their Dashiell Hammett."

"Raymond Chandler, actually," Monroe said. "Philip Marlowe."

"Nothing wrong with that."

"So, tell me," Monroe said. "How'd you enjoy the party?"

"We had fun," I told him. "Wasn't really what I was expecting but it was …" I trailed off, searched for the right word. Couldn't find it. "Damn good mojitos," was the best I could manage.

Monroe gave a knowing laugh and shook his head. "It's cool," he said. "I know what you're thinking. You expected better, bigger. The Hollywood party that you see in the movies. George Clooney and Brad Pitt in one corner, smoking cigars and drinking tequila. Julia Roberts and Jennifer Lawrence in another corner, discussing the difference between acting and producing. Martin Scorsese and Steven Spielberg in the hallway, talking about art versus commerce." He stopped and gave me a wink and a grin. "And I have parties like that, at my home in Beverly Hills. This just wasn't that kind of party. This was my B-party. People that aren't exactly Hollywood Royalty."

"Thanks for asking me to your B-party," I said with a playful smirk. "Now I know where I stand."

"Next time," Monroe said, and laughed. "Wait till we get this movie finished. You're gonna be a household name."

"I can't wait."

"What's on our itinerary for today?" Monroe asked.

"Today we're going to shake things up," I told him. "Ruffle some feathers."

"Oooh, sounds like fun."

"Yeah, you're not gonna think so," I said. "We're going back to the Lemon Grove Racquet Club."

"Why the hell would we do that?"

"Because I want to give that Archambault prick a little push. See what he does."

A hint of apprehension appeared on Monroe's face. "You sure that's the right thing to do?"

"It is now," I said. "Because we've got nothing else to go on. He told us to stay away from the Club … *or else!* … so we're going to do the opposite. See what happens when we push his buttons."

"What will that tell us?" Monroe asked. "I mean, we already know he's an asshole."

"It'll tell us how vested he is in this thing, whatever this thing is," I said. "If he ignores us, then it's probably nothing. If he comes after us, then there's something he's trying to hide." I smirked. "I may even ask him what he was doing at the Wilder's place. That'll send him into a tizzy."

Monroe wasn't sure. "I don't know," he said. "This seems a little risky."

I laughed. "It is," I told him. "But sometimes the risk is worth the reward.

Monroe grinned. "Okay. I'm in."

We got to the Club at just after a quarter to nine and there was no sign of Archambault or his Rolls. There were a few other cars in the parking lot, some that looked familiar, some not so much. I realized that Archambault might have brought one of his other vehicles, but I didn't know what those vehicles were. Powell could probably supply me with a list from the DMV but, so far at least, I didn't want to ask for the favor.

The Toyota pick-up was there, and the gardener was standing beside it, mixing water with what looked to be weed killer or perhaps bug spray. As always, he seemed to be the happiest person at the club.

Monroe sat in the passenger seat beside me, nibbling the remains of his McDonald's Bacon Cheese biscuit. Mine was long gone, the only evidence that it had ever existed the crumpled wrapper that I had tossed in the back seat.

Vehicles arrived and vehicles left. The two wanna-be tennis player/lawyers were out on a far court again, batting the ball back and forth like it owed them money. Despite the tennis ball violence, the morning was surprisingly peaceful and serene. Maybe the ridiculous membership fees were worth it after all.

Monroe was thumb-typing furiously on his phone when Archambault and his Rolls pulled in. Archambault worked hard on pretending he didn't see us at the edge of the lot as he pulled close to the building, climbed out of the mammoth car, and headed inside.

"This is where it gets interesting," I said.

"He didn't even see us," Monroe said, putting down his phone.

"Oh, yes, he did."

Ten minutes later the front door opened and Archambault came strutting out, his face plastered in an angry but somehow satisfied grin. Behind him were two big-shouldered men wearing t-shirts and windbreakers that had SECURITY printed across them in large, unmistakable, white letters.

"Stay in the car," I told Monroe, and opened the door of the Camaro.

"Good morning, gentlemen," I said, as the trio approached.

"Fuck your good morning," Archambault spat. He stopped about ten feet from the front bumper of the Camaro and his goons came to a halt behind him. "You're on private property. Trespassing. And I suggest you get the fuck out of here right now."

"Why?" I asked. "We're not causing any trouble. We're not in the way."

"It doesn't matter, asshole," said the big goon on the left side. "This is private property. We don't need a reason to ask you to leave."

"Maybe not," I said. "But it would seem like the polite thing to do."

Archambault growled. "Are you gonna leave?" He asked. "Or are we gonna have to throw you out of here?"

I frowned. Took a deep, cleansing breath. "You're probably gonna have to throw me out of here," I said.

I heard a car door open and looked over to see Monroe standing outside of the passenger side. *Goddammit*, I thought, *I told you to stay in the car.* Monroe was not a mind reader. He threw me a quick wink and stood there with his arms crossed.

"Okay, have it your way," Archambault said. He and the guy on his left came toward me. The other guy went for Monroe.

Archambault was easy. I popped him in the chin the second he came within reach, and he went down like a sack of whale blubber. The other guy, however, had a few inches and a few pounds on me and he had probably been trained to fight. I stepped into him and tried a punch to the right temple, but he jerked his head and my fist glanced off with little effect. He returned fire with a blow to my shoulder that numbed the upper half of my body and threw off my balance.

On the other side of the car, I heard Monroe gasp and cry out in pain.

The big guy came at me again but this time I was able to dodge his body blow and throw an uppercut beneath his jaw. His teeth came together in a gritty crunch, and I could see that I'd caught him off guard. He may have been trained to fight but he wasn't expecting to encounter someone who could fight back. He was probably used to pulling drunken rich people off each other after an argument about whose stock portfolio was worth more got out of control.

He took another swing at me but now he was off balance from my uppercut, so I stepped aside and it missed me completely. I jabbed him straight in the nose with everything I had and, from the pain exploding in my hand, I knew he was going down. He did.

And then the third guy was behind me, grabbing me around the shoulders and gripping me in a bear hug. He trapped my arms at my sides and I couldn't get my legs beneath me. I leaned my head forward and then jabbed back hard feeling a blast of pain and a sharp coolness as the back of my skull cracked into the guy's mouth. His grip relaxed around me, and I spun around, popping him once in the jaw and only relaxing when he wobbled and went down.

Suddenly, it was completely silent. The only sound were the insects in the trees surrounding us, the plop-plop of the lawyers playing tennis and the heavy breathing of the men on the pavement around me.

I raced dizzily around to the other side of the car. Monroe was there on his back, eyes closed, his face covered in a splash of blood. What looked like part of a tooth was balanced precariously on his lip.

I opened the car door and slipped my arms beneath his shoulders, lifting him. My left hand was screaming in pain.

Monroe's eyes popped open, and he blinked and let out a tiny moan.

"You're gonna be okay, tiger," I said, and shook my head. "I told you to stay in the car."

I loaded him into the Camaro, made sure the seatbelt was clicked, then ran around to the other side and climbed in. Seconds later, we were headed out of the parking lot. In the rearview mirror, I could see the three man we'd left behind getting groggily to their feet.

And then they were gone, and in their place was by nothing but a trail of dust and a road with eucalyptus trees on both sides.

CHAPTER THIRTY

"He broke my fucking tooth," Monroe said, staring into the mirror built into the sun visor. "Chipped the hell out of it."

"I told you to stay in the car," I admonished. "I could have handled those guys myself."

Monroe laughed and then winced in pain. "Well," he said. "I wanted the entire experience."

That made me laugh, too. "I guess you got that, all right."

He pulled a paper napkin out of the McDonald's bag and wiped the blood off his upper lip and chin. He winced, crumpled the napkin, and stuffed it back into the bag.

"Seriously, you okay?" I asked.

"Hurts like a bitch," he said. "But I'll be all right."

I looked down at my hand. It was already swollen and starting to turn a weird blue and yellow color. The back of my head was wet where the second security guard's teeth had cut my scalp, but it wasn't a huge cut and the bleeding had already stopped.

"So, what did we learn?" Monroe said after a moment. "And it better be worth it."

"It just may be," I said. "Archambault's onto us …"

"We knew that already."

"… and he's scared enough to come at us with violence. He didn't have to come out there with two security guards. He could have just called the cops and we would have been escorted peacefully away. He chose to put the fear of God into us."

"Did he?"

"Put the fear of God into us?"

"Yeah."

"Not exactly."

"And?"

"And now we know that whatever Archambault is hiding, he's serious about keeping it hidden."

"You mean like an affair with Mrs. Wilder?"

"Maybe," I said. "Although his visit to their home yesterday indicates that he just doesn't give a shit about who knows anymore."

We pulled into the Pierpont Inn parking lot, and I stopped the Camaro at the front entrance.

"Go clean up and get some rest," I said. "Get something to eat, maybe. Take Mongo to the pier, get him some tacos."

"What are you going to do?"

"I'm going to do the same thing," I said. "But probably without tacos."

"And then what?"

"And then I'm going to call our client and make an appointment to spend some time with him."

"Why?"

"I want to find out what he knows about Rutherford Archambault. See his reaction when we mention the name."

Monroe nodded. "Okay. When?"

"I'll call him today," I said. "Set up an appointment for tomorrow. Meet me at the office at the usual time."

"Got it."

He opened the door and climbed out of the Camaro. I watched him until he went inside. His walk was a little wobbly but not too bad. I thought he would be okay.

Then I headed home.

I followed Sanjon Road to East Thompson and turned right. My hand was really starting to throb now, and the back of my head felt like someone had taken a bone saw to it. A hot shower and a bag of frozen peas sounded pretty good right now. I passed fast food joints, auto dealers, a drug store, a car wash, and dozens of other businesses. East Thompson was a long road and there were a lot of them. As I approached Howard Street, the brake lights of the cars ahead of me flashed on and everyone came to a stop. I peered ahead and saw a crossing guard standing in the middle of the road, the octagonal red STOP sign held high over his head as he guided a line of school children across the busy road.

Broad-shouldered and barrel-chested, the crossing guard towered over the elementary age kids that were crossing before him. I couldn't see his eyes through the mirrored police-style sunglasses he wore, but it seemed from the movements of his head that he was constantly scanning the traffic for signs of danger.

He stood in the center of the street, sign raised high, until the last child climbed up onto the curb on the opposite side. Keeping the sign over his head, he started to walk back to his side of the street.

Two cars ahead of me, a black SUV suddenly accelerated, the driver apparently trying to pass through while the crossing guard was still in the middle of the street. But the guard stepped out in front of the car instead and it locked up its brakes in a haze of smoke and screaming tires, coming to a stop just inches from the crossing guard who didn't so much as flinch.

"The sign still says STOP," the crossing guard bellowed in a voice that I clearly heard three cars back. "That means you STOP until the sign comes down. That's the law!" He glared hard at the driver, daring him to take his foot off the brakes again.

But the driver simply lifted their right hand, and offered a meek "I'm sorry," wave.

The crossing guard held his gaze for one more second, and then walked off the street, keeping the sign held up high until he was safely up on the sidewalk.

Despite the pain in my hand and the back of my head, I found myself laughing and shaking my head. As the cars ahead of me moved on, I turned onto Howard Street and parked on the street near a used car dealership. I got out of the car, crossed the street, and then approached the crossing guard on the corner. He was sitting in a folding lawn chair, a newspaper open in front of him, and sipping something from a stainless-steel Yeti tumbler.

I walked up and gently kicked the back leg of the folding chair. The man looked up sharply.

"Gus Teague," I said, smiling brightly. "How the hell are you, you old dog?"

CHAPTER THIRTY-ONE

Teague told me he was off duty in fifteen minutes and asked if I'd join him at the Wendy's just down the street so we could catch up. I told him I'd get us a table and followed the sidewalk past Will Rogers Elementary School to the lot that contained both Wendy's and a Big Lots.

I ordered a large Coke Zero and a small order of fries and took a table in the corner. While I waited for Teague I nibbled on fries and massaged my shoulder where the security guard had hit me. Probably was gonna end up with a bruise there, too. I compared my two hands and was a little alarmed at how much my left hand was swollen. I was going to need those peas sooner rather than later.

But nothing was going to stop me from catching up with my old friend, my mentor, Augustus Teague.

About twenty minutes later, Teague walked in, scanned the restaurant, and gave me a wave. He went to the counter, ordered something, and came my way with a cup of coffee. I could see the printed image of a little red-haired girl staring at me through Teague's enormous fingers and wondered if that was Wendy.

Teague set his coffee on the table and wedged his massive body into the booth. He'd put on a few pounds since I'd last seen him, but he still looked solid and strong. He stood at least four, maybe five inches taller than me, and had shoulders that were some of the broadest I'd ever seen. When he took off his sunglasses, I could see that his eyes were clear and alert.

"Back of your head is bleeding," he said casually in his deep, gravelly voice. "Saw that out on the street." He glanced down at my hand. "That hand needs some attention, too."

"Had a little spat with a couple of security guards this morning," I told him. "You should see the other guys."

Teague laughed. "Yeah, that's what they all say. But, from what I remember, you probably did all right."

Teague was being charitable. The fact was that he had been the one who had taught me how to fight, as well as pretty much everything else. I'd worked for him for almost five years, first as an assistant, and then as a partner, and he'd taught me the ins and outs of detective work, plus the best way to defend myself. "You don't wanna get in a fight," he had said back then. "But sometimes a fight comes to you."

"So, you're a crossing guard now," I said.

"I had to do something," Teague said. "I was so god-damn bored. Sitting at home all day, watching too much TV, drinking too much beer. Swear to God, man, I almost got caught up in the soap operas. Christ, I was watching "Ellen" every day."

I laughed.

"Maybe you should never have retired," I said.

"Pshaw. That's a gig for the young. I'm 70 years old. Can you see me trying to chase down a perp?" He waved that thought away. "Anyway, I ran into an old friend who was doing this," Teague continued, tugging at the fluorescent orange vest stretched tightly over his barrel chest. "And it sounded okay."

"Working out for you?"

"Oh, yeah," Teague said. "Not a lot of hours, kids are great. And some drivers are assholes. Gives me the chance to shake 'em down a bit."

He took a sip of his coffee and looked at me. "What's up with you? Anything new and exciting in the gumshoe world?"

"Nah, more of the same," I said. "Currently working a cheating spouse case and a possible domestic violence."

"The usual."

"Pretty much."

"How's Marina?" Teague asked.

I frowned. "Not so good," I told him. "Her mother passed away recently and she's having a tough time with it."

"That's a tough thing to go through."

"It is."

"Tell her she's got my condolences," Teague said. He glanced down at my hand again. "God, that looks like it smarts," he said, giving his gruff laugh. "So, what's up with these security guards?" he asked.

I told him everything, from the moment Mr. Wilder came into to my office until our violent mamba with Archambault and the security guards. I told him about Shale Monroe, film producer and my shadow. I told him about Puño and Cassandra and my conflicted feelings on that front.

Teague listened intently to every word I said. He had always been a good listener. Said that was a tool of the trade. When I was finished, he took a sip of his coffee, stared soberly across the table at me and said, "Jesus, boy, you really know how to complicate a simple cheating wife scenario."

I laughed and reached for a fry. Realized they were gone. Sipped some Coke Zero instead.

"What's your next step?" Teague asked.

"Gonna call my client and set up a meeting," I told him. "Find out what he knows about this Archambault."

"Waste of time," Teague said. "And a little dangerous, too."

I raised my eyebrows. "Really? Why?"

"Even if he knows this Archambault guy, he's not going to tell you. He's just going to assume that that's the guy who his wife has been shtupping and he'll probably go after himself."

"He doesn't seem the type."

"None of them do," Teague said.

"So, what would you do?" I asked.

"I'd spend more time on the wife," Teague said. "Follow her all day for a few days, maybe a week. See where she goes, what she does. Get a feel for her schedule."

"And what is that going to tell me?"

"It's going to show you where the holes are," Teague said. "Where she's got free time and what she does with it." He drained his coffee cup and put it back on the table. "See, if she's got Pilates three times a week, and book club on Tuesdays and goes on a nature hike with her girlfriend from church on Thursdays, there's only so much time for extracurricular activities. And then, one day, you think you're following her to spin class and she ends up at Motel 6 with her legs up in the air."

"Makes sense," I said. "You know, I was actually planning to do that yesterday but got side-tracked."

"Get your legs up in the air?"

"No, smartass," I said. "Follow the wife."

Teague harrumphed. "Yeah, sure you were."

We talked another fifteen minutes and then Teague told me he had to get going.

"Got a gun safety course at the college at four," he said.

"You're taking a gun safety course?"

"No, stupid. I'm teaching it."

I did feel stupid.

We stood and shook hands.

"It was good seeing you again, old dog," I said, and meant it.

"You too, gumshoe," he said. "Don't be a stranger. Give me a call when this all shakes out and fill me in." He winked. "I'm dying to know how it all turns out."

"Yeah," I said. "That makes two of us."

Teague laughed. "Go home and take care of that hand," he said, and walked out of the restaurant.

I gathered up our empty cups and wrappers, dumped them in the trash can by the door, and headed home.

CHAPTER THIRTY-TWO

It was almost a quarter to nine the next morning before I heard the outer office door open, and someone came in. It wasn't like Monroe to be late, and I was just about to rib him about being tardy when the inner door opened and I realized it wasn't Monroe. It was Mongo. And he was coming in hot.

The big man came straight for me and, before I had time to react, he'd grabbed two handfuls of my Cirith Ungol t-shirt and lifted me out of my desk chair, pinning me against the wall.

"You put him in danger!" he spat, his breath hot on my cheek. "He could have been hurt out there!"

My surprise turned to rage. What the hell did this guy think he was doing? I opened my hands wide and slapped my palms hard against his ears. He gave out a surprised "Oh!" and, for a moment, I thought he was just going to shake it off. A split-second later, however, the pain kicked in and he dropped me to the floor, his hands going to his ears.

I stood up and glared at him. "What the hell was that about?" I growled.

Mongo was still staggering a little, holding his ears and shaking his head, but he turned to me with angry eyes and said, "You know what. He could have been killed yesterday."

"What are you talking about? It was a little scuffle."

"They broke his tooth!" Mongo scowled. "They bloodied his lip."

"Yeah, well, they messed up my hand and the back of my head pretty good, too."

"You were supposed to protect him!"

I gave him a surprised look. "The hell I was," I said. "That was never part of the deal."

"He's a movie producer," Mongo said. "Doesn't know the first thing about real life. About being in a fight. You should have kept him safe."

"Whoa, whoa, whoa," I said. "He's the one wanted to shadow me. I never said I'd keep him out of danger. As a matter of fact, I told him it would probably be the opposite."

"He doesn't understand," Mongo said, and fell into one of the client chairs. It creaked dangerously beneath his weight. "He's always lived a sheltered life. He doesn't know what's out there."

"Ah," I said. "And that's where you come in."

Mongo looked up me and took a deep breath.

"How long have you worked for him?" I asked.

"All of his adult life," Mongo said. "His father hired me when Shale was twenty. I've been with him ever since."

I gave Mongo another look.

"He doesn't know you're here."

Mongo shook his massive head. "Of course not."

"So where is he?"

"I convinced him to take a day off," Mongo said. "Lick his wounds. Told him I'd come over to tell you in person."

"A text would have been nice," I said. "Would have saved me from boxing your ears."

Mongo sat there a moment, staring at me, looking smaller than he'd ever looked before. He was still one big mofo.

I sat down at the desk. "Look," I said. "Sometimes this is a dangerous business. I've been beat up, shot at, and stabbed. None of that is fun."

"I know," Mongo said. And I was certain he did.

"Monroe wanted to do the research," I said. "Find out what it's really like to be a private detective. I've given him full access, including the violent bits."

"He doesn't understand."

"He understands a little more today than he did yesterday. That broken tooth will remind him every time he looks in the mirror."

"He's having it fixed today."

"You know what I mean," I said.

Mongo dabbed at his ears with his handkerchief, seemed relieved when it didn't come away with blood.

"Sorry," he said, after a moment.

"Apology accepted," I said, opening the lower righthand drawer. "Whiskey?"

He nodded.

I poured us each two fingers of Makers Mark and slid a glass over to his side. He took it and sipped, made the appropriate appreciative face. I sat back and drank a little of mine.

"Can you promise me," Mongo asked softly. "That you'll keep him safe?"

"I can't," I told him. "I don't know what's going to happen next. None of us know what's going to happen next. So, I can't make that promise. All I can do is say that I'll try."

Mongo sighed and took another swig. "Then that'll have to do."

"You care a lot about him, don't you?"

Mongo smiled. "He's like a son to me."

"I get that now," I said. "And I'll keep it in mind."

Mongo stood, swallowed the rest of his Makers Mark, and set the glass back down on the desk. "See you tomorrow," he said, and reached out to shake my hand.

I took it and gave it a solid pump. "See you tomorrow," I said.

Mongo turned and went out the way he came and, just like that, we were BFFs.

CHAPTER THIRTY-THREE

As agreed, Marina was home from work by two-thirty and we climbed into the Camaro together to head out to Millicent's place. She lived in a mobile home park out on the West End, *Rodando a Casa*, which Puño had told me translated to "rolling home." Cute.

I hadn't been to Millie's home in many years and, in fact, only once when I was working with Powell on a runaway case. I had chosen to wait outside while Powell went in, and Millicent did her psychic schtick. Things hadn't worked out that time—the boy was never found—but Powell told me that Millie had panned out several times before, once very spectacularly.

Millicent had been in her mid-60s back then which made her early 70s now.

We entered the mobile home park and drove through the narrow streets, making left and right turns until we came to Millie's home, located deep in the bowels of the park. From the outside, it looked like any another mobile home. Painted a pleasant turquoise and trimmed in white, the home had a spacious front porch with an aluminum awning and a pair of quaint metal benches on each side. A three-step stairway led up to the porch, with what looked like a handmade guardrail on the left side. A metal pipe windchime hung on one side while, from the other, swung a hummingbird feeder, its red contents being quickly sucked out by the pointy beaks of what must have been dozens of little birds.

I parked the Camaro in front of the home and killed the engine. We sat quietly for a moment and then I took a breath and turned to Marina. Her face was drawn and tired. "You sure you want to do this?" I asked her. "It's not too late to change your mind."

Marina stared at the mobile home for a moment and then slowly turned to me. "I'm sure," she said quietly.

We stepped out of the Camaro and walked to the porch. When we reached the bottom of the stairs, the front door opened and Millicent's daughter, Lenora, stepped out, her finger to her lips, indicating we should be quiet.

It was always somewhat jarring when one encountered Lenora. Her skin was baby powder white, and her long flowing hair was the color of newly fallen snow. It glistened vibrantly, almost translucently, in the sunlight. She looked down at us with metallic blue eyes that shown vividly through her alabaster eyelashes and finally took her hand away from her mouth and silently beckoned us inside.

Marina and I walked up the steps and followed Lenora into the home. The lights were all off and the shades had been drawn but it was bright enough for us to see how *homey* it all was. A clock with a face shaped like a cat's head adorned one wall. A crocheted throw was spread over the sofa. A modestly sized flat screen TV hung on another wall. In one corner sat a bookshelf, its individual shelves sagged with the many paperback volumes stacked thereon.

A glass of what looked like lemonade sat on a coaster on a coffee table, alongside a pair of remote controls.

The scent of burning incense hung loosely in the air, neither heavy nor vaporous.

Lenora closed the door behind us and came closer, her finger to her lips again. "She's preparing," she whispered, leaving her finger in place. "We'll go inside in a moment."

I nodded, glanced down at Marina. Her eyes were wide with fear or wonder. I couldn't quite place which.

Lenora disappeared down the hallway only to return a moment later. "She's ready," she whispered, and beckoned us to follow. "Remember, no talking."

We walked down the hallway and into a room at the end of the hall. As we stepped in, I heard Marina give a small, almost inaudible gasp and my eyes grew wide.

We were in a bedroom at the back of the mobile home. Millicent lay on the twin bed set in the middle of it, her hands gripped together on her abdomen, her fingers interlocked. A torn strip of some sort of cloth was gripped between the fingers of her right hand. She wore what looked like an antique dress, light blue with white horizontal striping. A tall, scalloped collar encircled her neck, folded beneath her chin, and rose behind her head. Her eyes were closed and she seemed at rest. She might have very well been sleeping.

Three of the four walls of the room were covered with custom-made shelves and these shelves were filled with antique dolls. There were baby dolls wearing dingy pajamas. Glamour dolls wearing lacy dresses, their porcelain heads overflowing with what I hoped was fake doll hair. There was a soldier doll, wearing the uniform of a country that only he knew the location of. There were dolls with eyes that seemed to follow you wherever you went in the room. There were a couple of unpleasant clown dolls, one with a face halved from a harsh drop or blow to the head. And, on the lower shelf of the wall closest to us, sat a lone monkey, a pair of cymbals in his hands, an eager grin on his face as he awaited the winding that would set him to playing.

The nightstands on either side of the bed were laden with as many candles as they had room for. Their flickering wicks danced in reflections on the wall. I couldn't help but wonder how fast this place would go up in flames if one of them tilted and fell to the worn carpet below.

Lenora invited us to stand on the right side of the bed while she took the small wooden chair on the left. She produced a yellow legal pad from the drawer of the nightstand on her side, and then a pencil, of which she licked the tip before touching it to the paper.

"Shall we?" she said to Millicent. I realized this was their cue to begin.

For a moment, Millicent lay quietly there on the bed, her hands clasped, her breathing even. Except for the sound of the birds outside and the distant roar of a leaf blower, it was completely silent.

"A chair," Millicent said suddenly, and Lenora quickly scribbled it down on her pad. "Wooden back, leather pad."

She became silent again. I felt Marina look up at me but resisted the temptation to return her gaze.

"A doorknob," Millicent said. Her body remained completely still. Lenora wrote something on her pad. I assumed it was "a doorknob."

"Old," Millicent continued. "Worn. The front of it is shiny from use and reflects the light. The back, where it's attached to the door, is dark and … oily? I guess."

Lenora's pencil moved.

"A metal screen," Millicent said. "Thick wire. Big holes. Square holes. It's set into wood, I think. No, plaster. Set into a wall. Maybe a garage."

I glanced at Marina. She stared down at Millicent with eyes full of nervous wonder.

"A field," Millicent went on. "Wheat, maybe. Maybe just weeds. It's sunset, or early morning. The wind is blowing gently, not a gust but just a breeze. There's a road nearby. Pavement. Old pavement. In need of repair. The line in the middle is yellow but it's old and cracked."

Lenora had just finished writing all this down when Millicent suddenly stiffened, and her eyebrows climbed up her forehead. "A sign!" she cried. "A wooden sign. An old sign! It's broken and beat up, but I can see the letters. I can still read it."

She squinted, as though her closed eyes were trying to focus on something inside.

"Packing plant," Millicent said. "Oconomo Packing Planet, Santa Paula." Her voice took on a tone of triumph. "Yes! Santa Paula! Oconomo. O.C.O.N.O.M.O."

And suddenly she went limp, and her eyes snapped opened wide. She stared up at the ceiling, unblinking, as though sightless. It was as if her heart had suddenly given out and she had died right there before us.

Marina shot a worried glance at Lenora.

Lenora didn't seem concerned. She calmly finished writing down the spelling of Oconomo and then put the pad back into the drawer in the nightstand, the pencil on top of it. She stood and guided us out of the room.

"She's finished," she whispered to us as we entered the living room again. "Sometimes it doesn't take long." She indicated the blanket-covered sofa. "Please sit while she recovers. She wanted to speak with you."

We sat beside one another on the sofa. Marina's face was ashen, and her eyes looked hollow and haunted. I took her hand and gave her a reassuring smile.

"Would you like some lemonade?" Lenora asked. "Or chocolate milk? We have both if you have a preference."

CHAPTER THIRTY-FOUR

We turned down the offer of beverages (although ice-cold chocolate milk is always good) and Lenora once again disappeared down the hall toward Millicent's room. Nearly twenty minutes later, they both came out and walked down the hallway toward us. I noticed that Millicent was using a cane, which I didn't remember from my previous visit.

"It's good to see you, Brace Heller," Millicent said with a warm smile, slowly lowering herself into the easy chair opposite the sofa. "How have you been, young man?"

"I've been well," I told her. "It's been too long, Millie." You always called Millicent "Millie." She wouldn't have it any other way.

"It has indeed," Millie said. "What is it? Eight years?"

"Something like that."

A sad look crossed her face. "Unfortunately, most folks only come see me when somebody is lost or dead," Millie said.

I offered her a warm smile. "I promise to drop by again soon just for the hell of it," I said. "Maybe I'll bring beignets." Being a Southern woman, Millie had once told me she loved those.

She laughed like a little girl, as much at the mild profanity in my words as for the possibility of beignets in her future.

"And this must be Marina," Millie said, leaning sideways in her chair to look past me toward Marina.

"Yes," Marina said. "Thank you so much for having us."

Millie waved her hand as if to ward off the gratitude and her face softened. "I'm so sorry about your mother," she said. "Brace tells me she recently passed."

"Yes," Marina said softly. "About a week ago."

"There's nothing harder," Millie said. "I keep telling Lenora she's got to prepare for it, especially with me getting up there, but there's really nothing you can do to prepare, is there?"

Marina couldn't speak. Merely shook her head. No.

"Did you get anything useful?" I asked Millie, to try and change the tone of the conversation. "Sounded like that sign you mentioned might be pretty important."

"It might," Millie said. "And it might not. Sometimes I see things that have no meaning whatsoever, at least as far as I've been able to discern." She nodded her head at her daughter. "Lenora's got it all written up and e-mailed over to the police," she said. "They'll go through it, see if anything helps."

Marina cleared her throat and wiped the corner of her eye. "What do you see?" she asked. "How do you know what you're … you know … looking at."

"It's the oddest thing, honey," Millie said. "I hold something belonging to the missing loved one in my right hand and I just lie down and close my eyes. And things start appearing to me. You know, like in my mind's eye.

They just float out of the darkness and then fade away to nothing. That's why Lenora takes the notes. It helps me to remember what I see, and sometimes I remember smaller details later." She looked at me and gave me a sad smile. "That's how I found that boy for your friend, Lt. Powell," Millie said. "During a session just like this one …"

"A much *longer* session," Lenora corrected.

"Yes, a much longer session," Millie conceded. "During that session, all I had was a little boy's baseball cap, the missing boy's cap. And I saw a car, a vintage car, a collector's car. And I was able to see part of the license plate as well. I'll never forget it. It was a 1957 Ford Thunderbird, cherry red, and the license plate was black with yellow letters. The first three letters were BZM." She looked up into Marina's eyes and gave her a sobering smile. "The police used that information to find the little boy's kidnapper, and they were able to find him before any harm befell him." Her smile brightened. "It was one of the proudest moments of my life."

"I'll bet," I said.

"Of course, during that session, I saw a whole bunch of other things that were just nonsense," Millie chuckled. "I think one of them was a banana and another was some kind of goldfish."

"It was a koi," Lenora clarified.

"Yes, a koi!" Millie agreed and chuckled again. "So many silly things come to me. But some of them are very real."

"They may *all* be real," Lenora said. "We just don't know the why or the where of it all."

"This is true, this is true," Millie agreed.

"Where do these images … come from?" Marina asked tentatively.

Millie pursed her lips and shook her head. "I don't know, honey. They just come. Over the years, I've been tested, re-tested, and tested again and the scientists have never been able to find nothing." She laughed again. "They gave up on me eventually. Haven't heard from any of them for nigh on ten years now."

Lenora said, "Thank the Lord for that."

Millie smiled. "My Lenora never liked the scientists," she said. "Always poking and prodding on me. Didn't bother me none but, bless her, it about drove Lenora crazy."

We sat there in silence for a moment, and I could sense that Marina's mind was working. Another second or two passed. She swallowed, took a deep, slow breath, and asked, "Do you think your visions could be … I don't know … a message? You know, from another … world?"

My eyes went from Marina's face to Millie's. I wasn't sure how the old woman would react, whether with puzzlement, anger, or embarrassment. Instead, she offered a sympathetic smile and said, "Honey, I've been asked that question a million times in my life. Where do your visions come from? How do you get them? Why you, of all people in the world, why you? And my answer is always the same. I just don't know."

Her smile turned sad, and her face softened even more. "But I can tell you this," Millie said. "I don't believe they come from the dead. I don't think that lost souls are pushing images into my brain. I don't believe that our deceased loved ones are coming to me with answers only they can know." She used her cane to push herself back into her chair and looked at Marina earnestly. "I think it's far more clinical than that," Millie continued. "I think it's just something in my brain that isn't in most other folks. Maybe I was born with it, maybe it happened when I fell off a horse when I was a little girl. Maybe it's nothing at all and I've just been lucky once or twice. They say a broken clock is right twice a day, don't they? Maybe it's just that. Maybe my broken brain has been right once or twice."

Marina leaned forward in the sofa, her knees just touching the coffee table there. "No, I get that," she said. "I was only asking ..."

"You were only asking because you just lost your ma," Millie said softly. "And I understand that, honey, I really do. I would give anything, *anything*, to be able to talk to my ma even one more time. Even if just for a few seconds. Just long enough to tell her I love her." She cocked her head gently and looked into Marina's eyes. "But that isn't the way life works, honey," she said. "Not in this world, at least."

Marina sat back slowly, her eyes focusing on nothing.

"I know there are folks out there who say they speak with the dead," Millie went on. "But my experience is that those folks are grifters and criminals, only out to make a quick buck, at the expense of the grieving." She turned to her daughter. "Lenora, honey, would you get me a glass of lemonade after all? All this talking has left me parched."

Lenora stood and turned toward the sofa. "Anything for you two?" she asked politely. We shook our heads and she headed off to the kitchen.

"That girl is my everything," Millie whispered. She turned her attention back to us. "Have either of you heard of a gentleman by the name of James Randi?" she asked.

Marina and I shook our heads.

"Called himself The Amazing Randi, he did," Millie continued, questioning us with her eyes. We shook our heads again. "Randi was a magician and a skeptic," she said. "I say 'was' because the poor man passed away recently, God bless his soul. Anyway, for 40 years, Randi offered a reward of one million dollars to anybody, *anybody*, who could provide him undeniable proof that anything supernatural existed. Over those 40 years, he had a thousand people try to convince him. Psychics, dowsers, remote viewers. All sorts of so-called 'supernatural' powers."

Lenora returned with Millie's lemonade. Millie accepted it and took a generous sip. "Oooh, that's good, honey," she told Lenora. "Just the right amount of tang."

She put down her lemonade and looked again at Marina and I. "Thing is," she said. "In 40 years, nobody could offer the proof he'd asked for. Nobody. Everyone who tried, failed." She took another sip of lemonade. "Even for a million dollars."

It was silent again, each of us lost in our own thoughts. Then, suddenly, Marina let out a sobbing gasp.

"I miss my mom!" she cried, burying her face in her hands.

I put an arm around her, but it was Millie who used her cane to get to her feet and hobble over. She put her arms around Marina and held her tight.

"I know you do, honey, I know you do," she said, and I could hear the tears in her voice, too. "And that's all right."

CHAPTER THIRTY-FIVE

Afterwards, we rode home in silence. Marina sat in the passenger seat, her arms crossed across her stomach, her head down, her eyes lost in thought. We didn't exchange words until we were back at my place, and she got out of the Camaro and unlocked the Miata with her fob. Then, she came around the driver's side, gave me a quick kiss, and said, "See you tomorrow."

"I'll call you," I said.

"Tomorrow." She got into her car and drove away into the night.

It was after six with the last tinges of the day fading into the darkness of evening. It was probably too early to swing by Cassandra's house—that asshole Locke probably wasn't even off work yet—but I didn't feel like going inside just to be alone and I sure as hell didn't feel like grabbing some dinner by myself, so I spun the steering wheel around and headed the Camaro toward the 101 and the west side.

My usual place was available, so I parked the car and killed the engine. I looked across the street and realized that I had been mistaken. Not only were both Cassandra and Locke's vehicles parked side-by-side in the driveway but the two of them were there, too, tossing a basketball into the battered hoop hung over the garage door.

They weren't playing Around the World or Horse any other basketball game I could identify. They were just goofing off. Taking shots, dribbling, and ribbing one other when the ball missed by a mile. They laughed and giggled and seemed to be having a terrific time. To anyone passing by, they would have looked like the happiest couple to have ever walked the face of the planet.

I watched them until it got too dark to play and, after one terrible final shot, they fell into each other's arms. Their silly laughs eventually quieted down as Locke reached out and tenderly touched Cassandra's face.

After a moment, they were kissing, which turned into necking which turned into something that made me feel like a peeping tom. I was thankful when they finally got up off the pavement and skipped into the house.

I started the Camaro and headed home. Nothing more to see here.

Chapter Thirty-Six

The two M's showed up at the office the next morning at just past eight. Monroe, his face still a little swollen just below the nose, and Mongo, dressed to the teeth as usual.

Monroe had a box of Krispy Kremes which I happily relieved him of. Mongo, uncharacteristically, came into the office behind him, gave me a look and a nod, and then turned around and took his leave. I guessed that was as close to a "Good Morning" as I was likely to get from the big man.

"How you feeling?" I asked Monroe.

"Better," he said. "Better than yesterday, at least. Still sore."

"Yeah, me, too. Get your tooth fixed?"

Monroe pulled back his lips and showed me. You'd never know there had been any damage.

"Nice job," I said.

"Better be. Cost me a fortune."

He sat and we ate donuts, and we talked a little about what we knew. I told him about my conversation with Gus Teague and the advice he had offered.

"So, is that what we're going to do?" Monroe asked. "Follow Mrs. Wilder?"

I nodded. "That seems like the best idea," I said. "Gus was right. No cheating spouse case should be this complicated. Usually, it's a couple of photographs, deliver the bad news, and go onto the next case. This thing's gone off the rails, especially considering Archambault's reaction. If we follow Mrs. Wilder everywhere she goes, and if she's having an affair, she'll lead us right to it. If she's not, all we'll do is waste a week of Mr. Wilder's money. And that's how it should be, by the way."

"Makes sense," Monroe agreed.

I grabbed another donut, sat back in my chair, and looked at him. "Was this all worth it?" I asked.

"What?"

"All the boring stakeouts, getting your ass whupped, spending your every waking hour glued to my hip. Was it worth it? Did you really get anything that helped with your movie?"

Monroe laughed. "I think so," he said. "The fact is that your life is more exciting than you lead people to believe."

"Oh, please."

"No, man, it's true. Think about it. Even me. Big Hollywood producer, right? Yet most days I sit in my office, answering the phone, running numbers, putting out fires. The highlight of my day is when I go to lunch, and most of the time it's the same tuna sandwich at the studio commissary. That's why I love being on set. Gets me out of the office occasionally."

He snatched another donut out of the box and went on. "You, on the other hand, are out in the element," he said. "You're out there in the real world. And you're working with real people, not characters created by some writer in a tiny, dark bungalow out in Calabasas. There are no plot points, there is no story structure. It's just what happens is what happens. And you have to react to it. Quickly. I think that's pretty damn cool."

"That's all true," I said. "But, in my world, there are also real consequences. I catch someone cheating on their spouse, two lives are ruined. I take pictures of a guy on disability playing handball at the gym, he goes to jail. I carry a gun for protection but, if I shoot someone, they die. There's a lot of heaviness to my work. A lot of responsibility. You don't have to worry about that in the movies. It's fiction."

"That's what I'm talking about," Monroe said. "See, that's what I've learned. What you do isn't like the movies at all. It's not portrayed accurately."

"And you're going to change that?"

"I don't think I can," Monroe said. "Movies are supposed to be about escaping reality, not reproducing it. Can you imagine if every time someone got shot in a John Wick movie, you felt the actual pain of the wounds? The pain of the loss? I mean, the guy who got shot was probably an asshole, but he's got friends and family who loved him. What about their loss?" He chewed his donut, swallowed.

"No, I think we have to keep doing things the way we've been doing them," he said. "Leave reality up to people like you."

"Does that mean you won't be making a movie about the Shorts and Sandals Detective?"

Monroe grinned. "Didn't say that."

We sat and thought about movies and life and ate donuts for a while. Finally, I folded the box closed. "Okay," I said. "Let's go see what Mrs. Wilder's up to."

CHAPTER THIRTY-SEVEN

Following Mrs. Wilder was going to be more difficult than we had anticipated. Because some son-of-a-bitch had slashed all four tires of the Camaro, and keyed both sides from bumper to bumper. It sat sadly in its parking place on California Street, deflated tires puddled around its wheels, the scratches looking like scars on a beauty contestant's smooth cheeks.

"Shit," I said. It seemed the most appropriate expletive.

"Shit is right," Monroe agreed. "Who the hell do you think did this?"

I swallowed. Tried to push the anger back down my throat. "I know who did this."

"You do?" Monroe said, amazed. And then it dawned on him. "Oh. Archambault, right? That prick."

"Well, if he thinks this is gonna stop us, he's in for a big surprise." I pulled out my iPhone, called AAA, and was told the tow truck would be there in 45 minutes or less. "Once they get this off the street, we'll take a Hubcap back to my place and grab my other car."

Monroe gave me a puzzled look. "Hubcap?"

"Ride share." His look was still blank. "Don't tell me you've never taken a ride share. Uber? Lyft?"

Monroe shook his head.

I laughed. "Well, then, here's another new part of real life you get to experience."

The tow truck was five minutes early and it was only six minutes after the battered corpse of my Camaro had been hauled away that the Hubcap driver arrived. So, it wasn't long before Monroe and I were in the Camry and headed for the Wilder residence.

"We may have already missed her," I told Monroe. "It's almost ten o'clock. She may be out and about already."

"What do we do then?"

"We wait until tomorrow," I said. "And start over."

But good luck was with us. When we pulled onto Cobblestone Street, we could see that Mrs. Wilder's car was still in the driveway. We knew this because the license plate on her Toyota Highlander read MRSWLDR. I would have bet big money that Mr. Wilder's was MRWLDR. They seemed like that kind of outrageously cute and clever couple.

"I'm going to go knock on the door," I told Monroe. "You're going to stay in the car and wait for me."

"Why?" Monroe had learned not to argue with me, but he hadn't learned to stop asking questions. Which, once I thought about it, was exactly why he was here.

"Because she's way more apt to open the door if there's only one stranger standing on her porch rather than two," I said.

He nodded. "That's a good point."

I stepped out of the Camry and crossed the street toward the Wilder home. I had just reached the sidewalk when out came Mrs. Wilder, purse hung over one arm, keys in the other.

I had to make a quick decision. Was it better to stop and talk to her now? Or better to follow her and see what her day was like? To see if, perhaps, she had an appointment with Dirk Diggler at the No Tell Motel.

I kept walking. She looked up as I passed her driveway and gave me a little smile. "Good morning," she said.

"Morning," I replied, and kept going toward the end of the cul-de-sac as though I had business there. Behind me, I heard her Toyota start up and then reverse out of the driveway. I kept following my path, down to the end of the road, around the circular cul-de-sac, and then back toward the Camry. Mrs. Wilder's Toyota disappeared at the corner, headed toward Foothill Road.

I broke into a run and dove into the Camry, starting it up and pulling a tire-screeching U-Turn.

"I thought for a second you were going to talk to her," Monroe said.

"Thought about it," I told him. "Decided it might be better to see where she goes and what she's up to today."

We took Cobblestone Road down to Foothill and turned right. Fortunately, there was no other way Mrs. Wilder could have gone. A cement island and a traffic sign proclaiming NO LEFT TURN blocked that way.

We caught up to her quickly enough, turning left onto Victoria Avenue. She headed South on Victoria, and we were able to stay close enough not to lose her but far enough away that she wouldn't catch the tail. She passed through a couple of stop lights and then turned right into a parking lot where a Wal Mart, a Carl's Jr and a Trader Joes shared space.

Mrs. Wilder's destination was Trader Joe's. She parked in a spot some distance from the storefront, far enough away to diminish the chances of someone dinging her car door while she shopped. We pulled in and stopped a couple of rows over and I killed the engine. We watched as Mrs. Wilder got out, went to the back of the Highlander, opened the hatch, and took out a handful of re-usable bags.

"We just sit here and wait until she's done shopping?" Monroe asked.

"Unless you have a better idea," I said, and gave him a look. "You're not going to get out and introduce yourself to her, are you?"

Monroe laughed. "Nah. Not this time."

Mrs. Wilder was in the grocery store for about twenty-five minutes and when she came out the two re-usable bags she'd taken were now swollen with what I assumed were produce, organic foods and wine. She loaded them into the back of the Highlander and, just like that, we were on to our next stop.

We followed Mrs. Wilder to the post office, to CVS Pharmacy and to a Chinese restaurant where she didn't stay long enough to eat. "Maybe she bought a gift certificate," Monroe suggested. "Or maybe just got a takeout menu?"

She stopped at the Chevron at the corner and fueled up, while Monroe and I peered at her through a group of homeless people huddled outside the Jack-in-the-Box next door. Next, she hopped on the 101 freeway and headed to Oxnard, taking the Wagon Wheel Road exit, and entering the Esplanade Shopping Center. She parked near Nordstrom Rack and went inside. While we waited for her to complete her shopping there, our mouths watered at the scent of grilled onions wafting over from the nearby In-N-Out Burger.

Mrs. Wilder spent almost an hour in Nordstrom Rack and then came out to her car with a single bag that seemed anti-climactic when compared with the time she'd spent shopping. She started up the Highlander, hopped back on the freeway, and got off at Telephone Road.

She turned left and crossed under the 101 freeway, and we followed her a few blocks until she came to McGrath Street, flipped a U-Turn, and guided the Highlander into the parking lot of an industrial complex. Once again, she parked at a distance and walked across the lot to a store-front that was signed VENTURA WINE COMPANY / THE CAVE.

I parked the Camry a few spaces away from the main entrance and turned off the engine. I could see the entire storefront and a patio area in the rear-view mirror.

We waited.

Fifteen minutes later, the door to the patio opened and Mrs. Wilder came out, a glass of wine in her hand. She took a seat at a table with an umbrella and sat there in the sun, sipping at her wine.

"We gonna just watch her drink?" Monroe said. "Because, truth be told, I could use a nice glass of champagne myself, you know what I mean?"

"No," I said. "I'm going to go talk to her."

I opened the door of the Camry and climbed out but before I shut the door, I said to Monroe, "Please stay here. For the moment."

"Of course," Monroe said, looking hurt that I'd even ask.

I tried to appear non-threatening as I walked across the asphalt parking lot toward the patio. Mrs. Wilder looked up, and I knew she was watching me, even with those huge dark sunglasses blocking her eyes. I walked up, palms open, and leaned toward the railing that divided the patio from the parking lot.

"Mrs. Wilder," I sent gently. "Do you mind if I have a word?"

She shook her wrist a little and I looked down to see a tiny pistol cupped in her hand, right beside the glass of wine she'd been drinking.

"I think you better just keep moving," she said. "Before I call the police."

I raised my hands softly. "You got a license for that?" I asked her. "Because, if you don't, calling the cops probably isn't a good idea."

"What do you want?" she said, but the gun never wavered. "You've been following me all day."

Which hurt because, clearly, I needed to work on my tailing skills.

"I'm a private detective," I told her. "Bruce Heller. I'm working on a case."

"A private detective," Mrs. Wilder said. "You expect me to believe that?"

"It's true," I said. "I can show you my license, if you'll allow me to get my wallet."

She nodded. I reached into my back pocket, pulled out my wallet and retrieved my P.I. ticket. I passed it over the railing and Mrs. Wilder took it and read it carefully. After a moment, she passed it back.

"Okay, so you're a private investigator," she said. "So what? Why are you following me?"

"As I said, I'm working on a case," I said.

"What case?"

Which is the question I was hoping she wasn't going to ask but I knew it was the question she was of course going to ask. Either I told her the usual "private eye/client" privilege nonsense, or I told her the truth. That was the dilemma. Both options had their pros and cons but only one option would keep her talking to me.

"Your husband, Dylan, hired me," I said. "About a week ago."

"Dylan?" Mrs. Wilder asked, her brows furrowing. "Why would he do that?"

I sighed and made an apologetic face. "He wanted me to find out if you were having an affair," I said.

Her shoulders sagged and the gun drooped. Mrs. Wilder rested her elbows on the table and held her head in her hands, shaking it in frustration. "Oh, Dylan, you silly man, what have you done?" she said to no one in particular.

She dropped the gun back into her purse and took a healthy gulp of her wine. "Well, you'd better come in here and have a drink with me, Mr. Heller," Mrs. Wilder said. "We've got a lot to talk about."

I nodded and turned toward the Camry.

"Um, do you mind if I bring my friend?" I said.

"Who's your friend?"

"Well, he's a Hollywood producer," I told her. "He's been shadowing me doing research for his next film."

Mrs. Wilder's eyes didn't even blink. "Oh, what the fuck ever," she said, and drank the rest of her wine.

CHAPTER THIRTY-EIGHT

I asked Mrs. Wilder what she was drinking and she told me champagne. Monroe nodded and went inside, returning a few minutes later with a fresh glass for her and a couple of beers for the two of us. I was impressed with his choice: Dogfish Head Palo Santo Marron brown ale.

"What did Dylan tell you?" Mrs. Wilder asked. She took the proffered champagne without a smile or a thank you.

"Just what I said," I told her. "He was afraid you were having an affair."

"Did he say why?"

"Just that you'd been aloof and disinterested recently."

"And that the sex hadn't been great," Monroe added.

"Thanks for that," I said, giving him the eye.

Mrs. Wilder sipped her champagne and then smiled wanly. "Well, he's right about that," she said. "I have been … what'd you say? … aloof and disinterested lately." She turned her attention to Monroe. "As for the sex, that's none of your goddamn business."

Monroe raised his hands in an apologetic manner.

"But there's some things that Dylan doesn't know," Mrs. Wilder said. "Things that I can't tell him. Things that have interfered with my life for the past month or so."

"Like what?" I prompted.

Mrs. Wilder looked up at me and then took another sip of champagne. "I'm not sure I should even be talking with you," she said.

"Your husband is my client," I said. "Anything you tell me will be confidential." I realized that probably wasn't true, but it sounded good.

"Unless I tell you I'm fucking my pool boy," Mrs. Wilder sneered. "Then you'll run off and tell Dylan, won't you?"

"Are you?"

"Am I what?"

"Fucking your pool boy?"

"What? No! That was a goddamn example, you moron. I'm not fucking anybody."

"Okay," I said. "Then what makes Mr. Wilder believe you are?"

"Because he's a shit-for-brains moron, too, all right?" She took a quick nip of champagne and sat back, staring into space. Just when I thought she was done talking to us for the day, she sat forward and said, "Okay, here's the thing. I'm not fucking anybody, and that includes Dylan, or the pool boy, because I've got other things on my mind. Okay?"

"Okay," I said. "Like what? Maybe I can help."

She started to brush me off and then suddenly stopped and cocked her head. "You know, maybe you just can," she said. "You're a big guy, you can probably handle him."

"Handle who?"

"There's this guy at the club," Mrs. Wilder said. "The Lemon Grove Racquet Club. I'm a member there."

"We know," Monroe said, earning him another cutting look from me.

"Of course, you do," Mrs. Wilder said bitterly. "You've been private investigating me."

"Go on," I urged.

"There's this guy at the club, not a big guy but bigger than me, you know. And he's been flirting with me for years. The typical guy thing, you know. Trying to get me to go out for a drink with him. Telling me my ass looks good in those tennis shorts. Saying he wished I'd leave my husband so he could have me all to himself. That kind of bullshit."

She drank some champagne. I drank some beer. I bet my beer was better than her champagne. I thought she'd bet the opposite.

"Anyway, over the past few months, this guy has become a real asshole," she said. "I can't go to the club and have a drink by myself, you know, because he always has to join me. He shows up at my Yoga class and waits for me in the parking lot. Tells me how hot I look in my yoga pants. The other day, I get home from hiking with the girls, and he's parked there in the street, staring at me as I go inside. It's been even worse the past couple of days. Seems like every time I turn around, he's standing there leering at me. And he calls me. Late at night. And just hangs up."

"Why didn't you tell your husband?" I asked.

"Dylan? Why didn't I tell Dylan?" Mrs. Wilder laughed, flashing her perfect white teeth. "That man has a temper!" she said. "If I told him some guy was messing with me, he'd fuck him up. I mean, you've met him, right? He's a fricking powder keg."

I thought about the meek Mr. Wilder coming to my office and asking me to investigate his wife and the words "fricking powder keg" weren't the words I would have used to describe the man.

"He'd end up trying to kill that guy," Mrs. Wilder said. "Or, at the very least, get us in trouble at the club. I couldn't stand it if we got booted from the Club. Can you imagine? It would be so embarrassing!"

"I can only imagine," I said. "What about the police? Have you tried to get a restraining order?"

"Not without Dylan finding out," she said. "Didn't you hear what I just said? He'd murder the guy!"

Mrs. Wilder drained the last of her champagne and I took another delicious swig of Palo Santo. I glanced over at Monroe and gathered that he'd reached the same conclusion that I had.

"Let me guess," I said to Mrs. Wilder. "This guy's name is Rutherford Archambault."

Mrs. Wilder looked up, eyes wide with surprise. "Yeah," she said. "How'd you know?"

CHAPTER THIRTY-NINE

We didn't get back to the office until almost 5 o'clock. The November sun was already dimming, and evening was coming on.

Mongo sat on the bench outside the office, waiting patiently for Monroe's return. Puño stood beside him, cleaning his fingernails with a switchblade. It was quite the juxtaposition.

"You good to go, boss?" Mongo said, standing. He had about an inch on Puño, who eyed him cautiously as he rose. If it came down to it, my money was still on Puño.

"Yeah, I'm exhausted," Monroe said.

"Get some rest," I told him. "We've got a big day ahead of us tomorrow."

Monroe smiled. "Yes, we do."

I glanced over at the two big guys. "You both got some free time tomorrow? Might need some back-up."

Puño simply nodded. Mongo shot Monroe a look, who gave him a nod of approval.

"Okay," I said. "Meet here about nine,"

"See you then," Monroe said, heading toward the elevator. Mongo was just behind him.

Puño watched them go as I opened the office door. "Cute couple," he said, as the elevator doors closed, and my office door opened.

We went into the main office, and I fell into my office chair while Puño straddled one of the client chairs. "What's up with tomorrow?" Puño asked.

"Later," I said. "I'll tell you all about it. Let's talk about Cassandra."

"That's why I'm here."

"I've been out to their place three times in the past couple of weeks. Spent some time watching Locke at his jobsite. Would've been more but we had Marina's mother's funeral."

"I understand. Sorry I couldn't be there."

I waved his apology away. "No worries. Marina knows you would have been there if you could." I opened the lower right-hand drawer of my desk and came out with the bottle of Makers Mark and two highball glasses. "Whiskey?" Puño nodded. I poured us both a finger and slid one of the glasses across the desk.

"So, the first time I went out to Cassandra's, I got nothing. Didn't see anybody, heard very little. Seemed like a peaceful evening. Second time out, however, I witnessed an argument. I see him get a little rough with her."

Puño stiffened.

"He didn't hit her, not that I saw," I said. "But they were having a very loud argument in the driveway. He grabbed her arm. Twisted it. Hurt her."

Puño stared at me through terrifying eyes.

"And then the third time I went out, it was like they were the happiest couple on the planet," I told him. "Playing basketball there in the driveway. Laughing. Horsing around. They ended up in each other's arms." I hesitated but decided to push on. "They practically made whoop whoop right there in the middle of the driveway."

Puño made a disgusted and surprisingly hurt face.

"So, the answer right now is that I don't know," I said. "I saw him put hands on her once but the next time I saw them there were practically Disney birds flying around their heads, singing love songs."

I could tell Puño didn't like what he was hearing, but I could also sense that he understood the situation.

"You want me to stay on this for a few more weeks, see what else I can see, you know I'm willing to do that," I said. "Might be a good idea."

Puño was quiet for a moment as he mulled over the information I'd given him. He sipped his whiskey, swallowed, and slowly shook his head. "Nah, man. I don't think so," he said after a moment. "Probably best for me to stay out of Cassandra's life anyway. We'll leave things be, for now. But I'll tell you something …"

"Yeah?" I prompted.

"I find out he's beating her, she won't be seeing him no more."

"How can you possibly control that?" I asked.

Puño gave me a menacing smile. "Won't *nobody* be seeing him no more," he said.

CHAPTER FORTY

The four of us met at nine the next morning and piled into Monroe's big Mercedes. Mongo was driving with Monroe sitting shotgun. Puño and I shared the backseat.

"This thing's like a damn private jet," I said, admiring the high-tech dashboard, the lush interior, and the overall fine workmanship.

Monroe turned around in his seat to face us. "Mongo picked it out," he said. "I figured he should be the one. I mean, he's the one who drives it, right?"

We pulled into the parking lot of the Lemon Grove Racquet Club at about 9:31 and parked as far away from the Clubhouse as we could. Mongo backed the big Mercedes into a spot with the skill of a professional driver (which, as Monroe had said, I guess he was). He rolled down all the windows and killed the engine.

I opened the bag that Marina had given me and passed everyone a string cheese stick and a fruit juice box. They gave me the glares that I probably deserved. "Don't judge me," I told them. "These are gifts from the wife."

We ate our string cheese and drank our fruit juices with the tiny plastic-wrapped straws that come glued to each box. Nobody said a word.

Thirty-five minutes later, Rutherford Archambault drove in, and it did my heart good to see he was in the Rolls. As usual, he pulled into the space closest to the front door, climbed out and walked straight into the building. I was pretty sure he hadn't seen us.

"You all done with your juice boxes?" I asked. Instead of verbal replies I got two glares and one extended finger. "All right then," I said. "Let's go in."

Five minutes later, we walked through the front door of the Club—the very door that boasted a stamped metal sign that boldly proclaimed MEMBERS ONLY—and approached the reception desk. The pretty young woman there looked up at us with a puzzled but friendly smile.

"Good morning, gentlemen," she said. "How can I help you?"

"We're here to see Rutherford Archambault," I said. "His friends call him Ruthie."

"Oh, so you're friends of Mr. Archambault?" she asked.

"Well, not for long."

She gave me another puzzled look. "I believe he's breakfasting in the dining room," she said. "But I'm afraid I can't let you go back there without a member escort. Would you mind?" And she held up the telephone.

"No, please," I said. And waited.

She dialed a three-digit number, and I heard a voice buzz inside the receiver. "Charlie? Hi, it's Anna. Um. There are some gentlemen here to see Mr. Archambault. Is he in the dining room? Would you ask him to come out, please? Thanks." She hung up the phone and turned her attention back to us. "He should be out in a minute," she said. "Have a seat, if you'd like."

"We'll stand," I said, and gave her a bright smile.

We stood. Monroe aloof and somehow still tense; Mongo still and immovable; Puño coiled like a snake ready to strike and me, well, I just crossed my arms and waited for Ruthie to arrive.

It took longer than I expected but, when I finally saw Archambault coming down the hall, I knew why. The two big security guards Monroe and I had met a few days before were behind him, their faces locked in grim visages of threatening power, some of which dissipated when they locked eyes with Mongo the Human Mountain and Puño the Hispanic Horror.

"What the hell are you doing here?" Archambault bellowed as he came closer. "Anna, call the police. These men are trespassing."

I saw Anna give him a quick, wide-eyed look, and then she glanced at us nervously and picked up the receiver.

"That won't be necessary, Anna," I told her. "We won't be here long."

Her eyes shifted to Archambault, and he nodded. The receiver dropped back into the hook.

"I'm just here to give you this," I told Archambault, and passed the tri-folded paper in my right hand over. He took it without a moment of hesitation, probably bolstered by the presence of the beefcake behind him and the fact that he'd only been sued—and, hence, served—twice in his lifetime.

"What is this?" he said angrily, unfolding the paper and briefly scanning it.

"It's a restraining order," I told him. "You're required to keep three hundred feet from Mrs. Kathryn Wilder for the next three weeks. That's a football field, Ruthie. And there's a court date set after that and, at that point, it might go on even longer."

Archambault looked up at me with eyes that spat pure hate, glanced down at the restraining order, and then quickly tore it in two, dropping both halves to the floor.

I frowned. "Doesn't matter if you tear it up, Ruthie," I said. "It's still legal, and you still have to stay away from Mrs. Wilder. Which means when she comes to the Club for lunch or a glass of wine, you have to leave. You have to be three hundred feet or more away. You can't be here when she is."

He gave me a look that he said he didn't believe a word I said.

"Really, that's how it works," I told him cheerfully. "I asked. If you don't leave, she can have you arrested." I gave him another happy smile. "I guess you can go outside and play pickleball or something, But you can't be in the building when she is."

"You piece of shit," Archambault said between clinched teeth.

"The other thing I wanted to tell you," I continued, "is that while that restraining order is good and legal, it's not the only thing keeping you away from her. There's also us." I swept my hand to my side, indicating Mongo and Puño. Neither of their faces changed but Puño's expression, even behind his big Ray-Ban sunglasses, would have melted steel. "If we get word you've been harassing Mrs. Wilder again, if you even *speak* to her in a cross way, we're coming back. And, trust me, Ruthie, that is something you don't want to happen."

I turned my attention to the two security guards standing behind him. "You two don't want that to happen, either." I could tell from their confused expressions that they did not.

I bent down, picked up the two halves of the restraining order, and handed them to Anna. "Anna, would you do me a favor? Scotch tape this back together and give it to Mr. Archambault later. He's going to need it."

Her eyes wide, her movements slow, Anna took the paper from me and looked around her desk for some tape.

"You all have a nice day, now," I said and the four of us turned. I could hear Archambault's heavy breathing behind me as he tried to control his rage.

At the main door, I stopped, put my hand on the knob and looked back. Archambault was still standing there silently, glaring at me with eyes that desperately wanted to shoot killing lasers through me. The two security guards stood behind him, looking as though they wished they were anywhere else.

"There is one more thing," I said, opening the door and standing back as Monroe, Mongo and Puño passed me. "And I probably should have mentioned it earlier." I smiled. "Your Rolls is on fire."

And I slipped out the door.

Outside, the first thing I heard was the brittle crackling of flames and the ticking of heated steel. A roiling cloud of black smoke billowed away into the morning sky as flames danced like raving demons in the Rolls Royce's windows. The entire cabin was filled with hungry fire and the windshield had cracked down middle. Black soot ran down the sides of the doors and something, probably the radio, burst with a sound like a gunshot. The heat coming off it felt good in the cool morning air.

I walked past the once classic car, crossed the expanse of the parking lot, and climbed into the SUV. Mongo already had the motor running and we were out of there in seconds flat.

Which still gave me time to see Archambault run out of the building, waving his arms, gesticulating furiously at the conflagration that was once his pride and joy, while the burly security guards raced up behind him, trying to handle a pair of huge fire extinguishers but managing instead to look like a chunky version of the Keystone Cops.

"Nice work, gentlemen," I said to the men in the SUV, once we were back out on the 118 and headed back home.

CHAPTER FORTY-ONE

Later that evening, I regaled Marina with my tale of bravado and stupidity, and she laughed at all the right places and *tsked* me at the other, more dangerous ones.

"What's to stop him from siccing the cops on you?" she asked.

"Nothing," I said. "But he won't. He fucked up my Camaro and I fucked up his Rolls. So now we're even. Plus, he's scared shitless of Puño and Mongo."

"Who wouldn't be?"

"No sane person," I said.

We were at the dining table, sharing ravioli and angel hair pasta from Presto Pasta. It wasn't absolutely authentic Italian food, but it was damn good anyway. Not for the first time, I wondered why they called it angel hair. I mean, nobody likes eating hair, right?

Except maybe Wurzel, who patrolled the floor beneath the table, searching for any errant food bits. Marina gave him a little piece of tomato and he sucked it down like it was the greatest ambrosia ever known to canines.

"If I may be so bold," Marina stated in a playfully authoritative tone. "You don't seem particularly happy that you solved this one."

I shook my head. "That's because I'm not," I said. "I mean, I'm glad the case is over and that we put together all the pieces, but I still feel like a shit-heel."

Marina blinked. "Really?" she asked. "Why?"

"Because I should have seen it earlier," I told her. "From the moment Mr. Wilder came to the office, all I could think about was proving that his wife was having an affair."

"Or not," Marina reminded me.

"Or not. But I never for a moment considered that Archambault might be a stalker. The signs were all there but all I did was try to prove, or disprove, an affair. I never even thought it might be a one-way thing."

"First of all, you didn't have all of the signs until you spoke to Mrs. Wilder."

"Yes, but …"

"Secondly, you were hired to find out whether she was having an affair," Marina said. "Not whether she was being stalked."

"Still, I have to wonder if I'd have done the same if it had been the other way around," I said. "If I'd been hired by Mrs. Wilder instead of Mr. Wilder."

"You can't think of it that way," Marina said. "Statistically, men are twice as likely to be stalkers as women."

"Be that as it may, I feel like I overlooked something. I feel like I let Mrs. Wilder down."

Marina took a tiny bite of bread and shook her head. "This is the way you have to think about this," she said, after she swallowed. "Mrs. Wilder wasn't your client, Mr. Wilder was."

I started to interject. Marina gestured for me to stop. "And maybe you should have seen the stalking clues earlier. Maybe you could have put it all together before everything came to a head. And maybe you didn't." She smiled brilliantly. "But you know what?" she continued. "You will next time. Next time you'll be thinking about it. Next time, you'll be aware of it. Next time, you'll explore that possibility along with all the other possibilities you already explore."

She reached out and tapped me on the nose. "Think of it as a learning experience, gumshoe," she said.

I just looked at her for a few seconds, took a sip of my wine, and then shook my head softly. "You are so full of shit," I told her.

Her laugh was magical and melodic.

"What about Shale Monroe?" she asked. "How much longer is he gonna stick around?"

"I think we're done," I told her. "After our adventure this afternoon, he said that he pretty much had everything he needs. Going back to Hollywood ... well, Calabasas ... tomorrow."

"And that's that?"

"Not exactly," I said. "He's stopping by the office tomorrow with some Krispy Kremes to say goodbye."

"Those are pure sugar," Marina reminded me.

"Those are pure Godly deliciousness," I argued.

We were quiet for a few moments, me chewing ravioli, Marina nibbling angel hair pasta. Wurzel got another tomato and almost jumped out of his black-and-white fur with the excitement of it all.

"How are you holding up?" I asked.

Marina chewed, swallowed, and thought for a moment. "It's hard," she said. "Seems like every day I see something in the paper or on TV and I think, 'I gotta tell mom about that.' And then I remember she's gone, gone forever, and it hurts like it did when I first lost her, you know?"

I nodded. Thought about my parents. Both alive. Marina was wrong: I didn't know. Empathy is one thing; reality is entirely another.

"But they say it gets better as time goes on," Marina continued. "And it does. It just takes so goddamn long."

I ate another piece of ravioli and chewed slowly. Wurzel looked up me expectedly, but he wasn't getting any of this. Tomatoes maybe. Ravioli, no way.

"Did you call your mom today?" Marina asked.

I shook my head.

"You should," Marina said. "You really should."

She was right.

I grabbed my phone, dialed my mom's house and we talked for almost an hour.

CHAPTER FORTY-TWO

Shale Monroe and Mongo the Human Mountain were sitting on the bench in the hallway in front of my office when I showed up the next day at 8:01am. Shale had not one but two boxes of Krispy Kreme donuts on his lap.

I unlocked the outer office door and held it open. As Shale walked in, I handed him a Coke Zero from the carryout tray in my other hand. He laughed and went on in.

Mongo stayed seated on the bench.

"Come on in," I told him. And handed him the second of three Coke Zero's.

He looked up at me with a smile of appreciation, took the soda, stood, and walked into the office.

We passed out donuts and drank our ice-cold beverages and sat there in the dim morning light, savoring the ocean breeze washing in through the open window above us and relishing a job well done.

"You think you got what you came for?" I asked Monroe.

"I do," he replied. "I'm anxious to get back home and start working on the script."

"Swell."

"Hey, you should be happy," Monroe said. "I finish this script and it's a guaranteed green light. I think that's another fifty Gs in your pocket."

"I'd have to ask my attorney."

"You don't seem very happy about that. What? You don't want fifty Gs?"

"Oh, I'll take the fifty grand," I said. "I'm just not sure how much I want to see myself portrayed on the big screen."

"Aw, you're going to love it," Monroe said. "By the time I get finished with this script, Brace Heller is going to be the biggest, baddest private detective in the history of the movies. Mowing down the bad guys, getting all the girls, solving crimes that the rest of the world only dreams about solving." He smiled. "We're talking to Brad Pitt's people. They say he's interested. Doesn't get better than that."

"Isn't he a little old?" I asked.

"How old are you?" Monroe responded.

I grinned and gave him the finger.

Monroe took a sip from the straw in his cup and stood. "It's been a blast, Brace, I gotta tell you. Wasn't what I expected, but I still had fun. Learned lots. And I appreciate your time and patience with me."

I got to my feet and reached out my right hand. Monroe took it and gave it a hearty shake. "It was better than I expected it to be," I said.

Monroe grinned. "I'll take that as a *I had a blast, too*," he said. "Mongo, let's get our asses home. I got work to do."

Mongo stood and extended his massive arm in my direction. I took the meaty claw that was his hand and gave it a shake. He didn't crush my hand in his, but I felt the power there. "Thanks for the Coke, Mr. Heller," he said. "Give me a call if I can ever be of assistance."

I stood looking at the big man with the big heart and I nodded. "I just might take you up on that, Jonathan."

"Mongo," he said, releasing my hand and smiling. "Call me Mongo."

A few moments later, I was alone in my office, sipping Coke Zero from a Chick-Fil-A cup and eating the last chunk of a Krispy Kreme donut from the sugar-stained box.

CHAPTER FORTY-THREE

It was about 2:30pm when the outer office door opened, and I looked up to see Dylan Wilder coming in. He still looked like the office nerd I'd met at the beginning of this whole mess and not the violently jealous killer his wife made him out to be.

"Mr. Wilder," I said. 'How can I help you?"

He walked up to one of the client chairs and put his hands on the back of it. He didn't sit down. "I just wanted to come by and thank you," he said. "For doing what you did."

"What, exactly, did I do?"

"Got that restraining order," he said. "Stopped Rutherford Archambault doing what he was doing."

I shook my head. "You misunderstand," I said. "I didn't do that. Your wife did that. She just needed someone to listen to her long enough to guide her hand."

Wilder nodded his head guiltily. "I know. You're right. I was too wrapped up in my own world to give Kathy the attention she deserved."

"Your world should include her," I told him.

"Oh, it does!" he said. "It does! She *is* my world, Mr. Heller. She's my everything."

"Make sure she knows that," I said. "Make sure to tell her. She needs to be know that she can come to you when shit like this happens."

"She does."

"She didn't," I said. "She was afraid of going to you. Afraid if she told you that this ugly man was harassing her that you'd go ballistic. Maybe confront him. Maybe blame her. It pushed her into a corner. Stressed her out. Depressed her. These last few months were a kind of living hell for her."

Wilder's shoulders drooped. "I didn't know," he said. "I didn't see. And I should have seen. I should have known."

"Well, now's your chance to make that right," I said. "Because Archambault isn't going to go away without a fight. He's a first-class asshole and those guys don't go away easily. You're going to have to be there for her and you're going to have to let her *know* that you're there."

"They kicked him out of the Club," Wilder said.

"They did?" I wasn't surprised. Private clubs hated this kind of attention and conflict.

"They did," Wilder confirmed. "And I hear it wasn't a pretty sight."

"I can imagine," I laughed.

"Anyway," Wilder continued, "I just wanted to let you know I appreciate your help. Whatever it was that you did, it's all for the better now."

I smiled. "I hope that's the case," I said. "Tell your friends. Referrals are usually the best new customers."

Wilder nodded. "I will," he said, and then turned around and walked out.

CHAPTER FORTY-FOUR

The one thing you should never do after closing a case like this is let your guard down. People don't like being caught doing something they shouldn't be. Whether it's a cheating spouse, an insurance scammer or a crime lord sleeping with his sister, putting their indiscretion on record is something most people don't take kindly to. There is always the possibility of repercussion.

I stayed late at the office that night, going over bills, checking invoices, and balancing my checking account. Considering the limited resources of my finances, it didn't take long. But Marina was out having drinks with the girls that evening and I wasn't ready to go home to sit on the couch and watch *Voyage to the Bottom of the Sea* re-runs with

Wurzel beside me, begging for whatever was in the silver tray of my TV dinner. Instead, I opened the Spotify app on my phone and sat back in my chair for a while, listening to AC/DC at a volume that would have chased off the neighbors if anyone else had been in the building at that hour.

I listened to a half dozen songs and, just as "Thunderstruck" came on I closed the app and stuffed the phone into my pocket. I mean, I love that song, but it's been played to death everywhere, and I mean *everywhere*.

The computer was off, and the fax machine was on (as if anyone sent faxes anymore) as I headed to the outer office door and pulled it open. My keys were in my left hand, and I was in the process of selecting the door key when I realized that someone was standing in the darkness just in front of me.

I had just enough time to register it was Rutherford Archambault standing there before he raised his left hand and drove the knife down into my chest.

There was a flash of fiery pain, and I felt the electricity of adrenaline explode inside of me. I tried to push my way forward, to fight back, but my body wasn't having it. I fell backward into the waiting room, my head glancing off the arm of a chair there, a new blast of pain blossoming at the base of my skull. The knife stuck out of my chest like a bad murder movie prop and then Archambault was on me, snarling, grabbing at the knife handle. He wrenched it back and forth, but it was stuck, trapped by ribs or muscle, and he couldn't pull it free to strike again. I tried to raise my arm to ward him off but couldn't make it move. It seemed dead and limp, worthless, and the world began to fade around me.

I knew that if I allowed that fade to go darker there would be no coming back, so I willed it away and took a deep breath. My chest felt as though a locomotive had driven into it at high speed and the back of my head was on fire, throbbing with pain in time with my now furious heartbeat.

Archambault sat astride me, eyes wide with crazed fury, drool leaking from his feral snarl. He jerked at the knife, shaking it back and forth, trying to free it from the gristle but it wouldn't come loose. I could only imagine the damage he was doing there.

That shadowy darkness came again. I tried to fight it off but this time it continued to grow and this time I knew I was going to lose the battle. The world seemed to turn into a storm cloud around me and its puffy grey pillows threatened to swallow me.

And then there was somebody peering at me from over Archambault's shoulder. Someone I knew. Even with a knife pressed into my chest and the world fading around me, I blinked my eyes in disbelief. My foggy mind told me it couldn't be.

But it was. It was Esmeralda. Marina's mother. Her kind, unmistakable face stared down at me over Archambault's shoulder with an expression of comfort and sadness that told me that, if it was time to let go, just go ahead and do it. Everything would be all right.

In direct juxtaposition, Archambault's sneering visage above me was filled with uncontrollable rage. *"Motherfucker! Motherfucker! Motherfucker!"* he screeched. He yanked at the knife again and this time it slid out of my chest with an audible squelch. A splash of blood left a gory diagonal line across his shirt and face. He squealed in unearthly triumph and raised the knife high above his head.

And then Esmeralda's face was gone, vanished as though it had never been there. And in its place was another face I knew, a face that made much more sense than Marina's dead mother.

It was Gus Teague.

And suddenly, Archambault was launched off me, as if tugged by monstrous marionette strings, and vanished into the darkness of the hallway. I heard a crash and a sickening crunch and then Teague stepped into the doorway and looked down at me with worried eyes. His cellphone was already to his ear.

"I got a stabbing victim at 21 South California Street," he said. "And I need an ambulance like goddamn now!"

CHAPTER FORTY-FIVE

I was swimming in the family pool. Underwater. And I wasn't holding my breath. It seemed natural. As though that was what I had always done, and what I would always do. I swam from one end of the pool to the other, enjoying the warm hug of the heated water and the freeing weightlessness of being submerged.

But I knew I couldn't stay there forever. As warm and as comfortable as I was, I knew that eventually I'd have to move on. And it seemed that the time was now.

I swam one more lap along the bottom of the pool, remembering how Dad used to throw pennies in so we could dive and bring them back up, and then I pushed my feet against the bottom and kicked, launching myself toward the surface.

I opened my eyes to find myself in a glaring white room. My chest hurt. There were cables and hoses attached to me in strategic locations. A hospital.

And Marina was there. She looked into my eyes and smiled. "Good morning, sunshine," she said, but not in the cheery way she would say it when were on vacation or one of those rare occasions when she'd slept over. There was a heavy tone of concern in her voice, of worry and cautious relief.

"How you feelin', gumshoe?" Gus Teague hovered into view, looking even bigger than I remembered him.

I tried to smile but felt my dry lips crack unnaturally. "Shitty," I managed to croak.

"I can imagine," Teague said. "Fucker came at you with a butcher knife. Big one." He held his fingers apart about ten inches in demonstration. "Rusty one, too. Prick."

"Archambault?" I asked. The name came out in three separate syllables.

"Yeah," Teague said. "Prick."

"Where is he?"

Marina shot Teague a quick look but either he didn't see it, or he didn't give a shit. I'd bet on the didn't give a shit. "In the County morgue, I think," he said. "Apparently, his pencil neck got broke when it hit the wall when I pulled him off you." He shook his head angrily. "Prick."

I was not surprised that I felt no remorse at the news of Rutherford Archambault's death.

"The doctor says you're going to be okay, honey," Marina said, leaning in and touching my face with her fingers. "There's some damage but he said it should heal quickly. You just need to rest."

"Three weeks, probably," Teague clarified. "Not bad for a stab wound to the chest. Good thing the knife was old and rusty. Dull as hell, apparently, too. Doc says it got stuck between your ribs. If it hadn't, you'd probably be sharing a slab down be in the morgue with Archambault right about now."

I saw the tears form in Marina's eyes and she lowered her head, pressed her forehead to my arm. "Oh, God,

Brace," she whispered. "I thought I was going to lose you, too."

That made me think of Esmeralda and brought back the image of her ethereal face, staring over Archambault's shoulder as he wrestled with the blade. A sense of warmth rolled over me.

"I don't think you have to worry about that," I said. "I think we've got someone looking out for us."

Marina pulled back, wiped tears from her cheeks, and looked at me questioningly. I gave her only a reassuring smile.

"Don't look at me," Teague said, raising his hands. "I'm not looking out for anyone. I saw your lights on, decided to stop by and see if you wanted to grab a beer. Didn't know you already had company. That prick." He laughed. "You're one lucky bastard," he said.

I looked into Marina's eyes. "I am."

Teague shook his big head. "All right. It's getting kinda mushy in here, so I'm gonna take off." He slipped into a blue LOS ANGELES DODGERS windbreaker and looked down at me. His hard eyes softened as he put a hand on my shoulder. "You need something, gumshoe, you give me a call."

"Thanks, Gus," I said. "I can't thank you enough."

"Got that right," he said, and was gone.

CHAPTER FORTY-SIX

Three weeks and four days later, Puño and I were sitting in his El Camino a couple houses down from a familiar home on Saratoga Street in Oxnard.

"How's the chest?" Puño asked. He was just making conversation. He'd been to see me almost every day since Archambault stuck the knife in me. He knew how the chest was.

"Hurts like hell," I said. "Doctor says its healing nicely, but it'll probably be three months before I can say it's healed completely. Sick of wearing this wrap, though, I can tell you that. Itches constantly."

"Fuckin' Archambault," Puño growled. "I wish Teague hadn't killed him so that I could kill him myself."

I laughed. It hurt a little. "I'm pretty glad Teague killed him," I said. "If not, I probably wouldn't be sitting here today."

Puño snickered. "Yeah, that's a good point." He touched the clock on the dash. "Two minutes to ten. Any second now."

"Any second," I agreed.

Almost exactly two minutes later, three Oxnard P.D. squad cars came barreling toward us, screeching to a halt at varying angles in front of the home with the worst yard on the street.

"It's going down," Puño said.

"I noticed."

Uniformed police officers spilled out of the cars and pushed past the gate, two approaching the front door and the other four holding back near the ancient GMC pickup that rotted in the middle of the dirt yard.

We couldn't see the front door from where we sat but, even from our vantage point two houses down, I could hear the thump, thump, thump of a police baton on a door and then a voice barking out. "Oxnard, P.D.!" A moment later, a jumble of voices babbled through the morning quiet, and it was obvious an argument was taking place. I pictured the asshole who'd taken Melissa Patterson's dog, and charged her $200 to get it back, standing at the door, telling the police they couldn't come in. That they would need a warrant.

I knew they already had a warrant.

I heard the front door slam shut and then there was a huge crash. The dog thief had probably slammed the door in the cops' faces and, in return, the cops had kicked the door in, warrant in hand. The four officers near the dilapidated GMC moved toward the house, out of our line of sight.

I thought of the poor dogs caged up in that front room. They must have been terrified.

"Wouldn't have been my move," Puño said beside me. "I would have sent two cops around back." He grinned. "Guess that's why I'm not a po-po."

A few minutes later, two of the officers came back out of the house leading a suspect in handcuffs. But it wasn't the asshole who I'd dealt with for Melissa but rather his girlfriend, or wife, or whatever the hell she was. They loaded her in the back of one of the squad cars, protecting her head like they do in all the movies, and slammed the door behind her. They returned to the house.

My eyes caught movement at the side of the house, and I looked over to see a man moving there, pushing past trash cans and hopping over the chain-link fence into the neighbor's yard.

"See?" Puño said, pointing. "Should have had someone covering the back."

It was the doughy man, the guy I'd dealt with, and it looked to me that he was wearing the exact same clothes he was wearing when I'd come to this house nearly two months earlier. I would have thought the dog-napping business would have been lucrative enough for him to own more than one set of clothing.

He walked through his neighbor's yard in what he probably thought was a calm, disinterested manner but that anyone with eyes would have called suspicious. The gate separating the yard from the sidewalk was closed and latched so the doughy guy opened it as quietly as he could, peering over his shoulder as he did so. He stepped out onto the sidewalk and walked coolly away from the police vehicles and toward us, as though he didn't have a care in the world. He tried to keep his eyes forward but occasionally turned his head and looked behind him, to see if perhaps he was being followed.

There was an old Volkswagen bus parked at the house in front of us and we watched as the guy peered in, hoping desperately to find keys dangling in the ignition. They must not have been there, because he quickly stepped away, glanced back nervously at the squad cars, and kept coming.

He passed the driveway of the next house and came toward the El Camino.

"What's this asshole doing?" Puño asked.

The asshole in question came closer and, I don't know if he didn't see us sitting inside or if he thought he was going to carjack us, but he came toward the passenger side, my side, of the car, and leaned down as if to talk to us through the window.

So, I threw open the door, hard, and smashed it like a hammer into his forehead. He jerked back like he'd been shot in the head and went down hard, his legs crumpling over the edge of the curb. I pinned him between the door and a tree in the grass there. A split second later, Puño was on top of him, his foot on the guy's shoulder. "Stay put, fuckhead," Puño snarled.

My chest was on fire. The effort had put pressure on the worst possible place, and I felt as though I'd just been stabbed again. I wasn't worried about the wound re-opening, but the muscle that had been damaged was screaming and yelling at me and calling me unrepeatable names.

As we sat and waited for the police to come take away the doughy man squirming in agony beneath the sole of Puño's boot, I found myself smiling despite the crushing pain in my chest. I thought of all those dogs locked up in wire cages stacked five high, underfed, mis-treated and filthy, and I thought of the shocked and pained face of the man responsible as the El Camino door had first crashed into his knees and then cracked him in the nose.

Wurzel, I thought, would be proud of me.

335

ABOUT THE AUTHOR

R. Scott Bolton lives in Ventura with his wife Shelley, his son Josh and his dogs, Zoey and Pretzel. He hosts several podcasts for fun, with topics such as showbiz and liquor, and you can listen to them by visiting his podcast studio at www.RoughEdgeFM.com.

Scott loves to hear from readers and welcomes e-mail at rsb@rscottbolton.com.

www.ingramcontent.com/pod-product-compliance
Lightning Source LLC
Chambersburg PA
CBHW061930170626
46813CB00006B/2352